Always, 'Twas You

by

Jennifer Moore

Always, 'Twas You

Cover Art by *Tina Lynn Stout*

The Wild Rose Press, Inc.
PO Box 708
Adams Basin, NY 14410-0708
Visit us at www.thewildrosepress.com

Publishing History
First Crimson Rose Edition, 2018
Print ISBN 978-1-5092-2249-0
Digital ISBN 978-1-5092-2250-6

Published in the United States of America

"I'm sorry I didn't believe you about the necklace."

"I'll not hold it against ye for bein' skeptical."

For a few moments, they were both silent. He thought she might have fallen asleep.

"Can you believe I did that?" she asked. "I climbed down from the tower?"

Her voice was softer and sleepy. He smiled at the pride in it. "I never doubted ye'd do it."

"I couldn't have done it without you."

His fingers trailed down her cheek, brushed around her neck, and threaded through her hair.

She shifted against him, her waist pressing against his hip, and a leg moving over his.

Heat spread through his blood.

In the tight space, she stretched out her arm, resting it over his chest.

His muscles jumped as her fingers moved along his side.

Her body melted into his. Again, she yawned. "Connor?"

"Mmm?"

"Thanks for coming for me."

His throat felt thick as he realized just how close he'd come to losing her. He squeezed her tighter. "I'll always come for ye, Katie."

Praise for Jennifer Moore

"What a fun read! THE SHEIK'S RUBY is a fabulous Cinderella story with both ancient and modern tones you don't want to miss."

~Josi Kilpack, author

"CHANGE OF HEART left me smiling and happy. Another great book from Moore."

~Amy Nelson

"SAFE HARBOR is a small-town romance to savor."

~Marilyn Baron, author of Landlocked

ALWAYS 'TWAS YOU was the first place winner of the LDStorymakers First Chapter Contest in the category: Romance/Women's Fiction

Dedication

For the Golden Pens: Josi, Nancy, Ronda, Becki, and Jody.
Your advice, critiques, and friendship mean the world to me.

Chapter 1

Your feet shall take you where your heart is.–Irish Proverb

The statue of Angus O'Brien loomed tall and proud in the great entry hall of Castle Hill Manor. The bronze image of the former lord rose over twelve feet high. Wearing a waistcoat, he proudly held his jacket lapels, forever frozen in the act of stepping forward. By a will's decree, Angus had ensured the figure of himself was placed directly across the hall from the main entrance to awe and welcome visitors to his manor house.

Centuries later, Kaitlyn Donovan stood at the top of the staircase, resting a hand on the carved wooden rail, looking at the statue from above. She wondered what Lord Angus would think about the modern additions of the reception desk which flanked him on one side, or the easel with the daily event schedule placed directly under his right elbow when her Uncle Seamus and Aunt Tillie turned the Manor House into a high-end resort. Based on what little she knew of the man, she didn't imagine he would be pleased with the abundance of visitors invading Castle Hill every week for their vacations.

From her vantage point, Kaitlyn scanned the room, and for a split second, her heart leaped when her gaze landed on a man leaning against the rail at the bottom of the stairs.

He'd shoved his hands in his pockets and crossed one ankle over the other, just the way *he* used to stand when he was waiting to meet her...

Kaitlyn shook her head. He was just another guest at the Manor Inn. Eight years had passed, she chided herself, and she needed to stop letting thoughts of Connor Flynn and his dark blue eyes haunt her here. Unfortunately, he was so tightly woven into everything about this place that he'd been creeping into her thoughts since she'd first arrived. Try as she might to replace those memories with new ones, they were not easily dismissed.

She turned her attention behind, to the windows in the upper hall. Stepping closer, she looked across the grounds. *Green* was the only word that came to mind. The vibrant color was nearly startling. She'd admired the view every day since her arrival but did not ever think she could become used to it. The very air seemed to shimmer. Although she hadn't been to Castle Hill Manor in eight years, the rooms and gardens felt as familiar as if she had never left. Her Irish blood must be the bond that kept her connected to this land.

Before turning back to the staircase, Kaitlyn caught a glimpse of her reflection in a gilded-frame mirror and finger-combed escaping curls back into her pony tail. Two weeks had passed since the funeral, and the mirror coverings had been removed, making the reception area look less somber. Glancing around, Kaitlyn smiled at the brightness.

The time since had flown by in a blur. Within twelve hours of receiving word of her Great Uncle

Seamus's death, Kaitlyn made a few phone calls and was on a plane to Ireland, arriving for the last night of his wake. Her eyes still prickled when she remembered Aunt Tillie's face and her warm welcome, in spite of the fact she just lost her husband of over fifty years.

Kaitlyn only met Uncle Seamus once. When she traveled to Ireland as a teenager. Kind and friendly, Uncle Seamus had been away on business more often than not. Over the years, Aunt Tillie made her few trips to the states alone.

The sound of the door closing caught her attention. Kaitlyn looked back down into the hall and toward the doorway.

Ian Kerry stood just inside the massive oak-paneled doors, his wide, smiling face turned upward. One hand held two tennis racquets. He waved with the other. "*Dia dhuit.* But yer lookin' grand today, Kaitlyn."

Kaitlyn was happy to see her friend. She skipped down the steps to join him. "Good morning, Ian." She smiled at his thick Irish brogue, loving the sound of it. "You look nice too." And he did. Ian Kerry had a classic, wholesome look—stocky and athletic with a square jaw and curling reddish brown hair that tumbled over his forehead. But hands down, his best feature was the bright smile which lifted his freckled cheeks and creased the skin around his gray eyes.

"I was beginnin' to think ye decided to mitch out on yer lesson today." He laid a hand on his chest. "I'm pure glad ye didn't. My heart couldna' take the rejection."

"Sorry. I guess I slept in a little." She accepted the racquet he offered and gave it a twirl.

"And a bit of a lie-in has done ye good. Yer eyes

3

are smilin'.""

In spite of herself, Kaitlyn laughed, and she batted her eyes a few times, just so he could see how smiley they were. Even though he was laying it on thick. The compliment was just the sort of thing an Irish man would say to an American tourist, but she didn't care in the least. She'd enjoyed spending time with Ian ever since her arrival, and their friendship was comfortable and easy. And having someone close to her own age to hang out with was nice, especially when he was handsome and flirty and seemed interested in her. So much time had passed since she'd had a date. What better way to get back into the swing of things than to spend her vacation with a fun, attractive tennis player?

As she walked past him through the front doors and stepped onto the gravel driveway that ran in front of the Manor House, she heard him chuckle. She breathed in the fresh rain-smelling air and admired the picturesque view of the Manor House grounds. Cottony bands of mist in the distance broke up the bright green of the grassy hills. The day was perfect.

"I hope ye don't mind, but after yer lesson, I've made arrangements to play a few matches with a mate and his *oul doll*. I'll be needin' a doubles partner, and y'are by far my favorite student." He nudged her with his elbow. "Would ye be for spendin' a few hours extra with me this mornin' then?"

"A friend and his what?" Kaitlyn frowned.

"*Oul doll*. His… girlfriend, she is."

She raised her eyebrows teasingly. "Ian, are you asking me on a date?"

"*Nil*, 'tis just a bit of tennis. Our *date* 'twill be this evening, if ye recall." He winked.

"I'd love to play doubles with your friends." She grinned, feeling excited at the opportunity. "As long as I'm back to meet Aunt Tillie by noon."

"Aye, and I'll be needin' to fetch Mrs. Wilkie for her lesson at half of eleven." Ian's mouth pulled in a small grimace.

She smiled at the expression. Apparently some of his clients were a bit too smitten by his brogue and flirting ways.

Ian took her hand in his as they walked down one of the shrub-lined paths that crisscrossed the estate.

Kaitlyn glanced at him from the corner of her eye. His boldness surprised her, but she had to admit, the attention felt good. Not good in the heart-pounding, tingling throughout her whole body way as when Connor had held her hand, but nice. And she wasn't a teenager anymore. Not every man she met would make her catch her breath or cause her to lose herself in his deep blue eyes. The time had come to grow up and stop believing in fairy tales. She'd make new memories at the Manor House. And turning to look at the friendly face of the man striding next to her, Kaitlyn decided Ian Kerry would be the perfect person to help her forget Connor Flynn.

Chapter 2

Connor unlocked the door of his Dublin flat and pushed it open, spreading the pile of accumulated letters beneath the mail slot across the wooden floor in the narrow hallway. He wheeled his suitcase through the entrance, closed the door behind him, and let out an exhausted sigh. Bending down, he gathered the mail, then stood, leaning from side to side to stretch his back.

The flight had been a long one. After a cursory glance around the sparsely decorated space, he saw everything was as he'd left it. As he walked down the hall that led to the bedroom, he rubbed his sore neck. He threw his keys on the dresser and then unloaded his pockets: wallet, passports, a handful of foreign coins, a few subway tickets.

He picked up his phone from the top of the dresser where it had sat for months in his absence and turned it on. Briefly, he scrolled through the list of missed calls. A few were from Tillie, but most were from his boss, Jack. Connor rolled his eyes. He'd call Jack later. He set the phone on his desk followed by his weapon. He took off his jacket then slipped the holster off his shoulders, feeling both physically and mentally lighter the more work-related trappings he removed from his person. As he shuffled through the mail, he glanced at his reflection in the mirror and ruefully scratched the beard he'd grown as part of his undercover disguise.

Exhaustion sapped his energy. A shower and shave would have to wait.

He tossed the pile of letters and magazines onto his desk, but one envelope in particular with familiar handwriting caught his eye. *Why would Seamus O'Brien send a letter by post instead of an e-mail or phone call?* Connor picked up the envelope, turned it over then tore open the flap, and stepped closer to the window to read with the morning light. Seamus's script was bold, like the man himself.

Connor,

I'm sending this letter in hopes of finding you well, my boy. I understand your mission could take some time, possibly months, and I'm afraid this communication couldn't wait for your return.

It's worried I am for my life. I pray to be proven wrong, but my fear is the secret we've kept for so long has been compromised.

Nobody on earth do I trust as much as you. To me, you have been like a son since you were a lad of eight years old, and your mother died in my employment. If my fears are justified, and my life is ended, I beg you to please keep the secret I entrusted to you. Do not let the relics fall into enemy hands.

I also beg of you to protect my dear Tillie. She knows nothing of this threat, and if I'm gone, she may become a target herself. I can't bear the thought. Please look after her.

I hope I shall see you again in this life, my boy. But if it is not to be, I pray the cause we have undertaken will continue dear to your heart, and I shall see you in the blessed hereafter.

Seamus

Connor looked at the date on the letter. Written over a month ago. The relics. The secret.

As the memory filled his mind, he rubbed his eyes. He'd been fifteen at the time and needing help with his school work. When he didn't find Seamus in his usual chair in the library, Connor searched the Manor House and heard a strange noise in the dining room. He found Seamus pulling back a large piece of the fireplace mantel to reveal an opening.

Seamus turned at the sound of Connor's gasp. "Come on, then, me boy." Seamus beckoned him closer. He carried a battery-powered lantern which he switched on and held over the dark hole, revealing a hidden staircase.

Connor followed him down the narrow stairs until they stood on the dirt floor in a dank, mildew-smelling space beneath the Manor House. The very air in the place felt old and stale.

Seamus indicated a bench against a side of the chamber and waited for Connor to sit before he sat next to him and handed him a small box. "Too long it's been that I've carried this secret alone, Connor."

At Seamus'ss direction, Connor opened the box and saw three golden pendants in the shape of different Celtic knots. Each was about the size of a large coin. He listened as Seamus told him a fantastical story about an ancient treasure and enemies who would stop at nothing to obtain it. Seamus admonished Connor to tell no one of the knots' existence and asked Connor to help him find separate hiding places for each of the pendants—relics, he'd called them.

At the time, Connor had felt as though he was humoring Seamus in a sort of superstitious family tradition. Surely, the tale had been only a legend. The entire incident was strange, Seamus was always so sensible. Why had he acted so paranoid regarding these *relics*? And 'twas equally unbelievable who Seamus had believed was looking for them.

Connor had not even thought about the objects for years. Seamus had only spoken of them in that one instance, and Connor assumed he'd either forgotten, or they were indeed unimportant. And the threat had been too far-fetched to even consider it valid.

Again, Connor read the letter, and worry churned in his stomach. Seamus wasn't irrational. He wouldn't have taken the precaution of writing to Connor unless he truly feared for his life.

Familiar enough with fear, Connor was used to controlling it. He usually had only his own life to worry about. Worrying the man he looked up to as a father might be in trouble caused a cold sensation of dread to spread in his chest. Not to mention the guilt which sprung up when he realized he'd have to tell Seamus what he'd done with one of the pendants.

Connor placed the letter on his nightstand. Just as he picked up his phone to call Seamus, it vibrated. Checking the caller ID, he sighed and lifted it to his ear. "Mornin', Jack."

"I've spent all night tryin' to reach ye. So, ye're back, then?"

Rubbing his eyes again, he sat on his bed. "I've just crossed me threshold, and ye'll be calling with a new assignment already, no doubt."

"The mission went smoothly, did it?"

"Aye, if by smoothly, ye mean I'm still in one piece." Connor slipped a hand around to rub the back of his neck. "I'll have my report on yer desk by Monday mornin', but as for now, I'm pure fatigued, so if ye'll excuse me..." He kicked off his shoes and lay back against his pillows.

"Actually, I've another reason for ringing ye, Flynn."

Jack let out a heavy breath Connor heard even over the phone.

"Seamus O'Brien is dead."

Pain punched his gut, and he sucked in a breath. He sat up, suddenly wide awake. A million thoughts filled his mind. He blurted out the first one he could actually articulate. "What happened, Jack?" His voice sounded high-pitched to his own ears.

"Preliminary findings suggest accidental drowning in his pond. But given his...um...former occupation, and the fact his private apartments and his office were both broken into the week before his death, the circumstances are under investigation. But we're keepin' it off the record until we know somethin' for sure. I'm not one for upsettin' a new widow until we've conclusive evidence."

Until he reached the window, Connor hadn't realized he'd started pacing. "The funeral?"

"Two weeks ago. I'm sorry. I know ye'd have liked to be there. How long since ye talked to him?"

"At least six months. Before this assignment." Connor spoke slowly, his mind not wanting to make sense of what was happening.

"Ye were deep under cover."

Jack's voice carried uncharacteristic sympathy, something Connor had never heard from the man before, and the sound made his eyes burn.

"I'd no way to notify ye until now."

As he thought of Seamus, Connor pinched the bridge of his nose between his thumb and index finger. Rust-colored hair graying at the temples and his ready smile. Was his death an accident? A coincidence? Or had a legitimate cause for Seamus's fears actually existed? Connor's gaze lit upon the letter. Was somebody searching for…he jolted upright. "Jack, was family at the funeral?"

"'Twas just his widow, Tillie, and a pretty lass from America. A niece, I think she is."

Connor crossed the room and typed on his computer, his pulse pounding in his ears. Clicking through the society column's pictures of Seamus O'Brien's funeral, he felt a constriction in his chest as he struggled with conflicting emotions. Worry, anger, fear…

A photograph of Kaitlyn filled the screen, and he caught his breath. *Katie*. She wore a simple black dress, and the camera had captured her at the precise moment when she leaned, eyes downcast to place a rose on Seamus's coffin. She'd cut her hair since the last photo he'd seen.

Her engagement photo, he reminded himself.

Connor enlarged the picture and found himself torn between the resurgence of old feelings her image stirred and the fear that she could be in danger. Leaning closer to the monitor, he studied her image. He clicked on the pendant hanging from a chain around her neck, enlarging it until no question was possible. Alarm surged through him.

"Ye know what they're after, don't ye?" Jack asked.

Connor had forgotten Jack was still on the line. "Jack, I'll be takin' a leave of absence." He rubbed his eyes, his mind racing. "I need to go to Tullybrae."

"Sure, and ye'll be needin' time to mourn. I know Tillie will appreciate havin' ye there." Jack let out a heavy breath. "Flynn, we both know what groups Seamus was involved with before he retired. Watch yerself. He was one of our best, and I don't need to remind ye of all people how serious this situation could be. I don't want to lose another good agent. The local *guarda* is investigatin' with our department, but we'll be the ones with jurisdiction. Any help ye need, they'll give ye. Ye'll call if ye smell any trouble, then."

If Jack only knew Seamus's true concerns, he'd be sending a team of agents to Tullybrae, but Connor made a promise to Seamus. He would keep his secret whether he fully believed its validity or not. He owed that honor to him. And he had to find out whether or not his death was an accident. Of course, Connor must take care of Tillie.

"Sure and I'll be careful, Jack. I'll ring if I've a need for assistance," he said before disconnecting the phone, gaze still glued to the picture. If he'd seen the pendant, the chances were good others had, too. And if 'twas the case, he needed to reach Kaitlyn before they did. He prayed he wasn't already too late.

Chapter 3

A few hours and a long drive later, Connor turned his car through the security gate. He stopped for a moment to speak to the guards and then drove onto the Manor House property. He'd taken the time to shower and shave and had even stopped for a quick haircut. Not because he might be seeing Kaitlyn, but out of respect for Tillie. She'd expect to see him well groomed.

Connor slowed the car on the circular drive, passing the stone fountain and pulling into the parking area near the putting green. Memories of his childhood at the manor, and of Seamus, were already thick around him. He took a deep breath and averted his gaze from the pond altogether. He was not ready yet to face the location of Seamus'ss death.

Opting to carry his suitcase rather than negotiate it on the gravel driveway, Connor strode toward the entrance and climbed the steps. But before he reached for the handle, he heard voices—one in particular stole his breath, and he turned.

Kaitlyn laughed as she walked up the path hand in hand with a bloke.

Connor wasn't prepared for the emotions that erupted inside when he saw her. *Calm yerself, man*. He had but a moment before she noticed him standing there and took the opportunity to study her.

The years had been kind to Katie. Her once-lanky

teenage body had filled out with feminine curves. He couldn't help but notice her shapely legs in the exercise shorts she wore. Her curling blonde hair was pulled into a ponytail, which swung back and forth with each step. And she walked with a confidence he'd not seen in her before.

As he studied her, the athletic-looking man, who Connor now realized wasn't the same man in her engagement photo, reached to take her racquet, pulling her closer until she bumped against him. He said something in her ear that made Kaitlyn laugh and swat his arm playfully. Connor scowled. Neither wore a ring. What was Katie playing at? Where was her husband? Why was she flirting with this man? Had she become a different person since she married?

The two of them were nearly at the door when Kaitlyn looked up and saw him. She froze, her mouth open and her eyes wide. "Connor," she mouthed, but no sound came out.

He took a few steps toward her, closing the gap. "Hello, Katie."

The man moved closer, as well. His eyes narrowed as he looked at Connor. "Who's this, then?"

Kaitlyn blinked when he spoke, shaking her head slightly. "Um, Ian, this is Connor Flynn. He's...an old friend. He grew up at Castle Hill." She waved a hand toward her companion. "And, Connor, this is Ian Kerry, the tennis pro here. But you probably know that fact."

The sound of her American drawl opened the door to a wave of memories, and Connor turned his attention to Ian in an attempt to distract himself. "I've not had the pleasure." He offered his hand.

Ian had to release his hold on Katie and shift the

racquets into his other hand to shake it.

Ian's grip was strong.

But if he thought a freckled tennis player wearing shorts and trainers would intimidate Connor, he was sorely mistaken.

"Hey, there."

The three turned when they heard a voice. A middle-aged woman wearing a pink velour sweat suit waved as she walked toward them. "Ian!" she sang. "Time for my lesson."

A flash of irritation crossed Ian's face, and he sighed before his face broke into a rather forced smile. "Sure and if 'tisn't the lovely Mrs. Wilkie. Ye'll be right on time as usual." He turned back to Kaitlyn. "Don't be forgettin' our plans this evenin'."

Kaitlyn's face colored. "Of course not. I'm looking forward to it." Her gaze darted to Connor, and then she looked back at Ian and smiled.

"As am I." He tapped his finger on her nose before walking toward his client. "Mrs. Wilkie, and if yer not the prettiest thing I've seen this day long, I'll be eating me racquet…"

Connor and Kaitlyn watched the two walk away, Mrs. Wilkie's bleached-blonde pouf bouncing as she chatted, and Ian nodding and smiling.

"A charmer, that one," Connor said, not intending it as a compliment.

Kaitlyn turned her head toward him and crossed her arms across her chest. "Oh, Ian is…yes…"

"I take it yer husband couldna' make the trip?"

"I'm not married, Connor," Kaitlyn said.

He could tell she tried to keep her voice casual, though her gaze darted away. She shifted her stance slightly, her discomfort evident. Guilt pinched his chest for the relief that washed over him at her words. *Time to change the subject, then.* "I'm sorry about yer uncle, Katie."

She rubbed her arms. "You missed the funeral. It was two weeks ago."

"I've only just returned from overseas."

Kaitlyn nodded, looking across the grounds at the green hills.

Why wasn't she looking at him? Was she so upset by her great uncle's death? Or was her reaction because he'd mentioned a husband? "I need to talk to ye about something, Katie."

She turned back toward him, raising her eyebrows.

He'd forgotten how deep and rich her brown eyes were, and a moment passed before he remembered what he'd intended to tell her. Before he could say anything, they were interrupted again, this time by Tillie, who had apparently come through the doors without his notice. That said a lot about the effect Katie had on him—he usually noticed everything. 'Twas his job after all.

"Connor, is it truly yerself?"

His throat grew tight. Connor stepped toward her and gathered the slight woman in his arms. "Tillie, so sorry I am about Seamus."

Tillie leaned back, looking up to see him. She placed her hands on the sides of his face. "My dear boy, yer here safe, and that 'tis a blessing."

He saw tears swimming in her eyes, but he knew she was putting on a brave front. Taking care of people was always her way of coping. "Aye, but 'tis late I am. The funeral is two weeks past."

"'Tis never too late to pay yer respects. And I'm grateful ye've come at last." She patted his face. "Kaitlyn and I are planning to visit the cemetery this afternoon if ye'd like to join us."

They both turned toward Kaitlyn.

She fiddled with the zipper of her jacket. She smiled when Tillie said her name, but the smile didn't quite reach her eyes, which widened at the invitation.

Connor wondered why the idea would bother her—surely she'd gotten over their teenage relationship long ago. She'd gotten engaged, for heaven's sake. Did she truly harbor ill feelings toward him?

Tillie reached toward her and Connor, grasping onto each of their hands.

"I would at that. But I'd not want to intrude." Connor studied Kaitlyn's body language. She was definitely uncomfortable.

"Maybe the two of you should go," Kaitlyn said. "I really have no reason—"

"Nonsense." Tillie pulled both of them closer and looked at them in turn. "It's decided. And we'll make a day of it. I've a need to spend some time with people I love. Besides, what's a trip to Tullybrae without visiting the cliffs, I'd like to know?"

Kaitlyn combed her fingers over the wavy strands curled around her face. "Um…I'd bette—"

"Ye go ahead and get yerself ready." Tillie had already turned toward the main entrance and spoke over her shoulder. "I'll take Connor to find something to eat. It's starved ye must be after yer drive. Breakfast is over, but the cook can find ye some bits and bobs. We'll all meet back here in an hour." She stopped at the open door and looked from one to the other, waiting for their acknowledgement of her plan.

Kaitlyn glanced at Connor one more time before she nodded to Tillie and walked past her through the Manor House doors.

"Come on, then," Tillie tugged at his arm. "Cook's been bakin' cakes all mornin'. Enough to feed an army, as usual." She led Connor through the great hall, past the familiar statue, and into the dining room. As they passed the kitchen door, she stopped to speak with a server.

Connor continued toward the table where he'd sat for nearly every meal of his life before he'd left for school. The familiarity of the surroundings made Seamus'ss absence more obvious. Connor was taken aback by the burning behind his eyes and the way his throat constricted when he saw Seamus'ss empty chair at the family table.

He swallowed hard and pressed his finger and thumb into the corners of his eyes. Feeling Tillie's delicate arm slip around his waist, he turned and embraced her. The slight woman was barely as tall as his chest, and hardly physically powerful, but not for the first time in his life, Connor relied on her strength.

The cook brought out a tray and set it on the table.

He cleared his throat. Connor pulled out Tillie's chair and once she was seated, he sat next to her and cleared his throat again, hoping his voice would not betray his emotions.

Tillie, ever proper, poured two cups of tea, placing one in front of Connor. She set down the tea pot, straightened her utensils, and blinked hard.

Connor slid a napkin across his lap. "And ye needn't be puttin' on a brave face for me. Tell me truthfully, how have ye been holdin' up?"

Before answering, Tillie took a sip of her tea. "I'll not lie. I have moments when I don't think I'll endure the pain. A hundred times a day I imagine I hear his voice or turn, expectin' to see him walk in the room." She dabbed her eyes with a white handkerchief before tucking it back in her sleeve. Her hands shook. "Sure, and I'm much better now that yer here, my dear. And I don't know what I'd have done if not for our Kaitlyn. She knows what 'tis to lose someone, does Kaitlyn, and 'tis a comfort to have her company."

Connor raised his eyebrows in a silent question as he took a bite of cake.

"Sure, and ye knew her ma died about a year ago. Her da moved away long before that, and then her engagement breakin' off so suddenly…" Tillie breathed out a sigh.

He leaned forward. "What happened, then? Between Katie and her fiancé?"

Tillie patted his hand. "Well, and 'tisn't me place to be spreadin' gossip. 'Tis Kaitlyn's story to tell, but I'll say, 'twas difficult and leave the matter at that."

For a few minutes, Connor ate in silence then wiped his mouth on his napkin. "How is the runnin' of the Manor House, Tillie? 'Tis overwhelmed ye must be, takin' it on yerself."

"Aye, a bit." She set her cup carefully on its saucer. "But I'm lucky. Ye know how Seamus was about keepin' perfect ledgers and records of everything. And he hired such fine people. I've not had to worry about anything o' that nature."

"I noticed when I pulled onto the drive that ye'd taken on extra security."

"Only temporarily. The measure seemed appropriate after the...accident, and nobody questioned it." Tillie glanced toward the kitchen then leaned closer, lowering her voice. "But I've actually another reason. We had a bit of an incident. And it involves dear Kaitlyn." She motioned with her other hand toward Connor's cup.

Connor's insides went cold. *Katie?* "What could Katie possibly have done that would cause ye to worry?" he asked slowly, sliding his cup toward her to refill.

"Of course 'tis nothin' *she's* done. But 'tis true, I've been worried. 'Twas the day after the funeral, Father McKenna rang me with a concern. Apparently, a pair of men—strangers, they were—came to him, askin' after Kaitlyn. Wantin' to know her name, where she was stayin', and things o' that nature. Her gaze narrowed. They were rather pushy, these men, and made Father McKenna uneasy."

As questions filled his mind, he rubbed the back of his neck. A knot of fear lodged in his chest. "Have ye heard any more about it, then?"

"No, I've heard nothin' since. I've not gone into town since the funeral, and Kaitlyn's been a darlin' about stayin' with me. And as an extra precaution, I've asked Ian—he's the new tennis pro—to keep an eye on her." She shook her head. "I've not spoken to her about the men, of course. No need to alarm her."

Must be the necklace they were after. He'd been right to come. Katie *was* in danger. "Ye trust this tennis player, then?"

"He's been nothin' but kind to her, Ian has. Every bit the gentleman. He and Kaitlyn have gotten on splendidly. She's taken a likin' to tennis, and he's asked for me permission to take her out tonight. 'Tis like I said, a true gentleman."

Connor said nothing. His mind was still spinning, and he doubted he could simulate kind words about the tennis lad.

The silence stretched on, and Tillie reached across the table to take his hand. "'Tis only a friendly outing, my dear. I'm of a mind that 'twon't take much to win back the heart of our Kaitlyn, if that's what's worryin' ye."

Connor prided himself on his ability to conceal his emotions. In fact, that particular skill had kept him alive more than once. So, he was always astonished by how easily Tillie could read him. On top of his embarrassment that Tillie had seen through him so easily, Connor gritted his teeth against a tinge of jealousy mixing with his anxiety. "Ye think she'll be safe with him, then?"

"We've had no cause for concern these past two weeks."

Thoughts running through various scenarios, Connor nodded. He needed to get that necklace from Katie, and he needed to protect her from whoever wanted it. This action was what he'd been trained for—defining the objectives of a mission and achieving them. As he calculated the safety measures he'd need to establish, his mind kept drifting, finding itself occupied with soft curling hair, a pair of deep brown eyes, and the feelings he'd tried to forget for the past eight years.

Chapter 4

Kaitlyn closed the bedroom door behind her. She walked on shaky legs to sit on the bed and kicked off her shoes then let herself fall back onto the pillows. Her chest tightened, and her stomach rolled.

Connor Flynn. She'd had no warning, and suddenly he was there: standing straight as a soldier with his notched chin, a jaw that appeared chiseled from granite, and those dark blue eyes that looked straight through her. Her mind went completely blank, and she'd opened and closed her mouth like a fish, making a fool of herself, of course. Kaitlyn pulled a pillow over her face, groaning at the memory of how ridiculous she must have looked.

What was he doing here now? The funeral was two weeks ago. She had braced herself for the chance of seeing him then and had even felt a twinge of disappointment when he hadn't been there. But afterward, she'd relaxed and hadn't even asked Aunt Tillie why he hadn't come.

Kaitlyn's skin tingled, and she felt panicky. Her fight-or-flight instincts were kicking in, and she considered throwing everything into her suitcase and taking the next plane back to Seattle. But no, of course she wouldn't. She breathed in and out, pulling down the pillow and clutching it against her chest. She was here for Aunt Tillie. Kaitlyn was the dear woman's only family, and she couldn't leave her at a time like this.

She sat up, pulled off her socks, and shrugged out of her jacket, throwing the pillow back into place before walking into the bathroom and turning on the bathtub faucets. Swirling her hand around in the churning bathwater to check the temperature, she shook her head against the image of Connor's face that popped up in her mind again.

Of course, Connor Flynn had become even more handsome. His thick hair was cut short now, spiking slightly, and without his curls, all trace of teenager was gone. The youthful roundness of his face had been replaced by masculine planes and angles. He looked like he'd just stepped out of a magazine, and Kaitlyn was certain ladies were lined up at his door.

The last time she'd seen him was eight years earlier on the morning she'd left. He helped Uncle Seamus load suitcases into the car, and after she hugged Aunt Tillie, Connor pulled her into his arms.

"'Tis only for a short time, Katie," he murmured. "I'll be thinkin' of ye every day." He touched the pendant he'd given her and tucked it under her T-shirt collar. Even with her parents and Aunt Tillie and Uncle Seamus watching, he rubbed his thumbs across her cheeks to wipe away her tears and brushed a kiss over her lips. "I love ye, Katie girl," he whispered. "And I always will. Never forget that. Never. 'Twill be but a short while before we're together again."

In a choked voice, she told him she loved him, too. Then, feeling as though her insides had been scooped out, she climbed into the rental car. Her last view of Connor Flynn was him standing with his arm around Aunt Tillie, waving goodbye as the wind blew his curls across his forehead. The image had been permanently branded in her mind, and whenever she missed him, she'd recall it.

But they hadn't been apart for a short time, as he promised. Instead, eight years passed. She didn't know what to make of those things he'd said back then but wished her heart could discard them as silly words from a teenage boy in puppy love with no concept of what her living in America and him staying in Ireland really meant. She wished she could erase the memory of Connor's curls, his kisses, and his promises.

As Kaitlyn realized how high the bath water had gotten, she started from her reminiscing. She forced her mind back to the present. Connor said today he needed to tell her something. That didn't sound good. Was he planning to tell her everything he'd said, all those promises he'd made years ago, were a lie? Did he think she still believed him? That she was pitifully waiting for him, and now he needed to make sure to set the record straight?

She'd spent the last eight years forgetting and pushing away the ache his memory still caused. Maybe this meeting was a chance to get closure on what obviously had been a teenage crush. Maybe being with Connor would help her to recognize her feelings for what they were—irrational. She twisted the pony tail elastic, pulling it free, and shook out her hair before rubbing her head.

Surely, nobody could be as perfect as she'd remembered him being. Undoubtedly teenage infatuation had glorified the entire relationship and put him up on a pedestal where no one else could ever compete. Now that she had another chance to spend time with him, she could look at him with mature eyes and force these skewed memories out of her mind. *I've moved on.*

Kaitlyn wouldn't make this day awkward for any of them. Three adults could pay their respects to a man they'd loved without making the situation uncomfortable. She was a grown woman, and she'd prove it by not reacting to Connor and his charms. One thing was for sure, she'd given him her heart once, and in no way would she trust him with it again.

After the quick bath, Kaitlyn blow-dried her hair, and she applied make-up. Which she told herself had nothing to do with seeing Connor Flynn, and everything to do with looking respectful for the cemetery visit. She grabbed her purse, and her gaze fell on the necklace on top of the dresser. She picked it up, feeling heat climb her cheeks when she remembered the night Connor had given it to her.

She traced the familiar pattern of the Celtic knot before gritting her teeth and fastening the clasp behind her neck. So what if she'd received it from Connor? That wasn't why she was wore it. She liked wearing it. He'd told her himself it had belonged to Seamus. And the pendant was a fitting tribute to her great uncle. She didn't care what Connor Flynn might think of her wearing it now. If he noticed, she could tell him point blank her wearing it had nothing to do with him.

Despite her justifications, she tucked it under the collar of her shirt anyway as she walked down the stairs. She wasn't sure she was ready for him to call her on it too soon.

Connor and Aunt Tillie stood in the entryway waiting.

As she approached, Kaitlyn avoided making eye contact with Connor and reminded herself again that she was over him. This occasion was her chance to prove the truth to them both.

"And yer lookin' lovely, my dear." Tillie turned and beamed at her nephew. "Doesn't she look lovely, Connor?"

"Aye, that she does." Connor raised his eyebrows and nodded slightly.

Kaitlyn wished she had control over her blush. She needed to rein in these reactions if she would handle being in the same household with Connor.

Tillie linked arms with her. "Shall we, then? Connor's just now brought around his car, and I'll never be one for turnin' down a ride in a fancy sports car."

Kaitlyn glanced up to see Connor watching her. Was he waiting to gauge her reaction to his expensive car? "That will be great," she said, stepping past Connor through the doors.

They walked down the Manor House steps toward the shiny silver vehicle which had been parked—rather ostentatiously, she thought—right in front. *How practical for the three of us—a two-door sports coupe.*

Connor held open the car door, and he and Kaitlyn looked at each other awkwardly for a moment before Kaitlyn realized it was the passenger door. Having the steering wheel on the other side was so disorienting. She noticed he glanced around. Was he making sure everyone noticed how great his car was? *Oh, brother.*

Insisting Tillie sit in the front next to Connor, Kaitlyn climbed into the small back seat, turning her legs to the side so she didn't bang her knees. She ran a hand over the soft cushion. It still had that new-car smell mixed with the aroma of leather and Connor's spicy cologne. She struggled against leaning back, closing her eyes, and taking in a giant sniff.

Connor pulled onto the gravel drive and turned to Tillie. "And tell me about the funeral, then."

"Oh, Connor, 'twas a grand procession. Had ye been here, ye'd have been a pallbearer, of course." Tillie laid her hand on her chest and drew in a deep breath. "The *guarda* stopped traffic, and even O'Malley's pub was closed for the day. Perfect weather 'twas—a soft, gentle rain. And so many of our dear friends walking through the town to fill the church yard."

Connor nodded, his gaze on the road.

Aunt Tillie turned slightly in her seat. "Sure, and, Kaitlyn, weren't the Requiem Mass and Father McKenna's eulogy truly perfect?"

Kaitlyn glanced toward the rearview mirror then turned to Tillie. "The service was beautiful. The wake, the procession, the funeral. And the people who came back to the Manor House after. The music, the food…well all of it. A fitting tribute to such a good man."

She had been overwhelmed by the beauty of the solemn Catholic ceremony. The traditions, the kneeling, standing, sitting, and especially all of the friends who gathered for days at the house, singing, laughing, crying, eating, and drinking. The comfort of the customs and the warmth of the community had touched her heart. A part of her longed for this feeling of belonging.

Kaitlyn worried with Uncle Seamus gone that Aunt

Tillie would be lonely, but not a day passed without people from Tullybrae paying the Manor House a visit. She was relieved her aunt had the support system to lean on, but she found herself feeling a bit jealous at the same time. Plenty of people back home she considered friends, but here, the closeness was more like family. A family was something Kaitlyn wanted so badly that it caused an ache in her chest.

The skin around Tillie's eyes crinkled in a warm smile. "And dear Kaitlyn. Aye, she's been such a help at the manor and such a comfort to me. Arrived just in time, she did. 'Tis lucky I am to have such great people as yerselves in me life."

Though the procession took nearly an hour a few weeks earlier, the drive through the town to the cemetery only took about fifteen minutes today. As they drove, Kaitlyn noticed Connor constantly scanning the sides of the road and looking in his rear view mirror. She wondered what had happened to make him so paranoid on the country road. They only passed one other car the entire time. Had he always been such a cautious driver? Maybe this behavior is what happens when one drives an expensive sports car. Rocks and potholes become problematic.

Once they arrived at the churchyard, Kaitlyn let out a breath of relief. She thought the backseat would be a good place to hide but felt exposed to his scrutiny when she'd glanced up to see Connor's gaze flick to hers in the mirror. She hated that he could see her so fully when she could only see his eyes.

Connor parked on the side of the small road and walked around to open Tillie's door for both women.

They walked through the short wrought-iron gates.

Kaitlyn couldn't help but remember coming here years ago with Connor and studying the headstones. Some were still recognizable, shaped like Celtic crosses or angels, with ancient names and dates carved into their pocked surfaces. Others were indecipherable lumps of crumbling stone worn away by the years and the weather. The older portion of the cemetery was overgrown with long grass hiding many of the black and gray monuments. However, the O'Brien family's section was well tended and located conveniently close to the gray stone church.

At the grave, Kaitlyn stood a little apart as Connor and Aunt Tillie talked about Uncle Seamus. For the first time in the weeks she'd spent with her, she saw Aunt Tillie's countenance crumple as she described the details of the service to Connor. As she watched the intimate moment, Kaitlyn felt like an outsider.

Connor stood with his arm around Tillie, head tilted, listening and rubbing her shoulder. Though not related by blood, Connor was every bit the child the O'Briens never had.

"Loved ye like a son, he did," Tillie said to Connor as she wiped her eyes with a lacy handkerchief. "Aye, and he couldna' have been any prouder of ye, Connor."

"He was the only father I ever knew. And I'll miss him dearly," Connor said softly.

The three stood silently a few moments longer, until Tillie turned, angling herself to face both Connor and Kaitlyn. She looked back and forth between them, squinting her eyes slightly. She tucked her handkerchief into her sleeve, and then told them she wanted to go meet the priest for confession. "Why don't the two of ye take a wee walk around the cemetery? Sure, and ye

must have some catchin' up to do. I shan't be long."
She gave Connor another hug, squeezed Kaitlyn's hand,
and then followed the gravel path to enter the old
gothic-style chapel.

At her aunt's obvious attempt to throw the two
together, Kaitlyn winced inside. She walked toward a
stone bench on the older side of the cemetery.

Connor followed.

She noticed he kept glancing toward the road. Was
he afraid someone would scratch his car?

"How's yer family, then, Katie?" Connor sat next
to her.

The yummy smell of his cologne swirled around
her. She ran a hand over the ancient pocked stone of the
bench. "I don't know if Tillie told you or not, but my
mom died last year."

"Sorry I am to hear that."

Her heart felt heavy at the memory. "My dad just
remarried right after Christmas and moved to Arizona.
So, I'm pretty much on my own now."

"Sure, and Tillie's grateful to ye for comin' to be
with her."

Kaitlyn swallowed and nodded. She looked across
the churchyard at the green hills, which were sectioned
off by stone walls. A few cows dotted the landscape
here and there, and she could barely see the ruins of the
old castle on the hill, nearly hidden by trees.

"Yer still living in Seattle, are ye?" Connor asked.

"Yep. Duvall, actually. The city's about a half hour
away. I teach third grade in a little school there."

"A teacher. Aye, that I can see. Ye've the right
disposition for the job."

"What do you do, Connor?" Kaitlyn turned to see

him watching her again. A bubble of warmth started to grow in her chest, which infuriated her.

"Nothin' so excitin'. I've a government job. But it pays the bills, sure enough." The side of his mouth lifted. "And how long are ye stayin' in Tullybrae?"

Kaitlyn fought against allowing her heart to melt at his half-smile. "Tillie invited me to spend the summer. So, about another month. Then I have to get back before school starts."

Connor nodded. He leaned forward to look past her toward the road, and then shifted to rest back on one arm, moving his gaze to her face.

Kaitlyn hated that he looked so intently. Or more like she hated that she loved how he watched.

He reached up and tucked a curl behind her ear.

The nerves in the side of her scalp started buzzing. She fought against the urge to close her eyes and lean against his hand. Was she really letting this situation happen again? Didn't she give herself a pep-talk before she left her room?

"Truly, I've missed ye, Katie." He again leaned back on his hand.

His hand was positioned closer this time. She could nearly feel the electricity between them, and an alarm went off in her head. *Time to get a grip.* "I've missed you, too. But us…together…that was a long time ago, and I'm sorry Aunt Tillie is making this reunion awkward—you know, playing matchmaker." She gave a small smile which she hoped appeared easygoing and casual.

Connor wasn't paying attention. He watched the road.

Had he even heard her? Katie stood and started

back toward the church. "Let's get going. I can tell you're feeling uncomfortable." *Is he expecting someone?*

Connor caught her arm, stopping her.

Heat from his touch spread over her skin as he studied her face.

Shaking his head, he took a breath and let it out slowly. "I've something important to talk to ye about."

As she looked up at his face, she pressed her lips tight and tried not to show the effect his touch had.

Glancing around, he took a step closer. Then his gaze dropped down to her neck. "Yer necklace." He frowned. "Ye musn't be wearin' it. I'm askin' ye to return it to me."

Kaitlyn gasped. She lowered her chin, shielding her face behind her hair and hoping he couldn't see the tears in her eyes. Was he serious? Her face burned. She jerked away her arm, fumbled with the clasp behind her neck, pulling on the chain, and pressed the necklace with its golden ornament into his hand. Any worries she'd struggle to convince herself that she'd indeed moved on vanished instantly. Avoiding Connor's gaze, she whirled and hurried toward the church, mortified.

"Katie, wait. I didn't mean—"

Kaitlyn wasn't listening. She spotted Tillie coming through the arched church doorway and headed toward her, wishing she could just continue back to the Manor House, to the airport, and home to Seattle. When she reached Aunt Tillie, her mind scrambled to think of a way to politely take a rain check on their plans.

Aunt Tillie's face lit up when she saw them. "Shall we, then?"

Kaitlyn knew she couldn't hurt Aunt Tillie's

feelings. If she stormed off in a huff, Connor would know how his request for the necklace had devastated her. He must have someone else he wanted to give the love knot to. But to take back the pendant after all this time...she jerked as if she'd been slapped. Eight years ago, she'd thought her heart couldn't hurt worse than when she'd said good-bye to Connor, but he had just proved that theory wrong.

Connor held open the car door. He touched her arm and tilted his head to catch her eye.

Kaitlyn turned away her face, not wanting him to see the hurt she couldn't keep hidden. She climbed into the back seat and avoided glancing at the rear view mirror, resigning herself to spending a few more humiliating hours with Connor Flynn. The back seat that earlier had seemed so comfortable and soft now felt cramped. Her stomach churned, and Kaitlyn couldn't help but hope he'd ding his pretty car on the rutted road leading to the cliffs.

Chapter 5

Made a right hash of that, I did. Connor looked into the rear view mirror.

Katie's chin trembled. Her arms were folded, and she focused on the view out the window through rapidly blinking eyes.

He'd messed up badly and needed to explain himself. How he fumbled for words around her and acted like a teenager was ridiculous. He was a grown man. An experienced man. A government agent who engineered and executed perilous operations. He could read people like a book, and he knew exactly how to manipulate any situation and any person. In fact, that skill was one of the reasons he was still around. Why was he letting her get under his skin? How could she still have this effect? He needed to stop being sentimental. This visit was a mission. Just like any other. She was a civilian in danger, and he had done what was necessary to protect her by reclaiming the necklace he should never have given her in the first place.

But a not-so-logical part of his mind reminded him she was also his Katie. The first girl he'd ever loved and the only one he'd never forgotten.

The drive was short. He and Aunt Tillie chatted nostalgically about Tullybrae and Seamus. Connor slowed on the rutted, rocky road and gritted his teeth at the damage the drive was undoubtedly causing his shocks. The car crested a rise that brought the ocean into view.

The dramatic landscape never failed to astound him—the powerful waves crashing against towering, sheer cliffs. From their vantage point, high on the craggy rocks of Carrick Point, he could see along the winding coastline and out across the water where dark humps of islands rose out of the blue ocean.

When he parked his car near the overlook, Connor blinked at the flash of memory that appeared. Years ago, he and Kaitlyn had ridden his old motorcycle to this very spot. Her hair was longer, and she wore it pulled back, held in place with pink hair clips. When they climbed off the bike, Kaitlyn stood away from the cliffs, chewing on her lip.

Connor coaxed her closer, reaching his hand toward her. "Come on then, Katie. Ye can't see anythin' from back here. Ye'll not believe how grand the waves are, smashin' against the cliffs."

Shaking her head, she wrapped her arms around herself. "I'm not going anywhere near that edge. Why isn't a guardrail or something here?"

"Hold my hand, I'll not let ye fall." Connor took her hand, noticing how soft and small it was. She was trembling. He smiled to encourage her and was met with a half-hearted smile in return.

"I know you wouldn't, but can we just watch from here?"

Her coffee-colored eyes were so big and so trusting. A warmth started in his chest and spread. He would never let her down. He'd squeezed her hand tighter and lifted it to his lips. "Of course, Katie. 'Tis every bit as lovely from here."

His mind snapped back to the present, and he thought about how much had changed in eight years. Connor's gut was heavy with guilt when he remembered the way Katie looked at him today when he'd asked for the necklace. He'd hurt her and needed to find a way to make their relationship right. He climbed out of the car and walked around to open Tillie's door, helping her out, and then leaned the seat forward.

Katie climbed out with jerky movements, ignoring his offered hand, and stepped to the side.

She was upset then or embarrassed. Most likely both.

Tillie held his arm as they made their way to the lookout point, and Connor wasn't surprised when Katie hung back.

Leaning her head against his shoulder, Tillie stood silently for a long time looking at the view. "Loved the sea, he did. Many a time he brought me to this very spot, and just like this, we stood and watched the waves, listenin' to the crashin' and just bein' together. He was a good man, me Seamus."

"Sure, and he loved ye very much." Connor patted her hand where it rested on his arm.

"I've no doubt. But I miss him somethin' fierce." Tillie turned.

Connor followed her lead. They walked back a few steps to where Kaitlyn stood, well away from the edge.

She gazed out at the water as a few tendrils of hair blew across her face.

Once he wouldn't have hesitated to brush them off her cheeks but knew she wouldn't welcome it now. And why did his mind even go there?

Kaitlyn closed her eyes and inhaled. Her face softened. "It's so beautiful." She opened her eyes and smiled at Tillie.

She didn't even look at Connor. He grimaced.

"Aye, that 'tis. I've always loved watchin' the waves crash into the cliffs. 'Tis somethin' grand about all that raw power, to be sure." Tillie looked from the sea back to Kaitlyn's face. "But 'tis pale ye are, me dear. Ye'll not be gettin' ill?"

"No." Kaitlyn lowered her head and folded her arms. "I'm fine. Just a little tired today."

Connor clenched his hands in his pockets in an effort to control the urge to reach out and lift her chin.

Tillie held onto Kaitlyn's hand. "Come, let's have a sit then, shall we?" She led them toward a bench carved into the stone and sat next to Kaitlyn, patting the seat on her other side for Connor to join them. "'Tis here me Seamus proposed. Right on this very bench over fifty years ago. So young and handsome he was, and I was powerful in love with him." She pulled the lacy handkerchief out from where she'd tucked it into her sleeve.

Her voice grew soft, and her eyes were distant as she looked at the ocean. Connor wondered whether she remembered they were still there.

"Aye. Sure, and there's nothin' in the world like being in love. And nothin' can give us such deep pain as when the one we love leaves us."

At Tillie's words, Katie winced. She wrapped an arm around Tillie and took the handkerchief from Tillie's hands to dab the older woman's eyes.

When Connor looked at her, her gaze slipped

briefly from Tillie's face and met his. Her gaze was full of pity and love for her aunt. Somehow in her quick glance, she had let down her guard, and he saw an expression in her dark brown eyes he remembered from years ago. An expression that made his heart turn over and his chest tighten.

Katie quickly looked away.

Was she still in love with him? Connor stood and rubbed the back of his neck. He couldn't be right. Not after all this time. He must have imagined the emotion. A combination of nostalgia at seeing her and the ache of losing Seamus must have made him misinterpret her fleeting expression. Although, he'd been nearly certain...

Tillie stood. "Well, and I've had a grand bout of self-pity today. I thank the two of ye for listenin' to an old lady's woes. But, 'tis time to be off. I've guests and a hotel to run." She brushed off the back of her slacks with a hand. "So, shall we then?"

She held onto Kaitlyn's hand, linked her arm through Connor's, and the three of them made their way across the stony ground to the car for the drive back to the manor house.

The ride was quiet. Each lost in their own thoughts. When they arrived, and Tillie climbed out of the car, she took Connor's hand. "And 'tis time for tea."

Kaitlyn opened her mouth.

But Tillie continued, linking her arms through both of theirs again. "Sure, and 'twill help ye feel better, Kaitlyn. 'Tis peaked yer lookin'."

As they walked into the dining room, Connor could practically feel the resentment coming from Katie. A few other guests sat at tables and couches spread around the room.

Kaitlyn avoided his eyes and made small talk with a British couple seated next to the outside doors while Aunt Tillie excused herself to make a phone call.

Connor sat at the family table.

When Tillie returned, she and Kaitlyn joined him, and a server brought cakes and finger sandwiches and, of course, a china tea service.

Tillie lifted the elegant tea pot that sat in front of her and poured tea for the trio. "Well, my dears, I'm afraid I'm in a bit of a jam. I'll be needin' to meet with Seamus'ss lawyer tomorrow mornin', and I've a bus full o' High Babies from Galway arrivin' for a tour of the manor house. Would the two of ye be willin' to show them around?"

"A bus full of what?" Frowning, Kaitlyn squinted her eyes.

"Children," Connor clarified. "Young school children. High Babies, they'll be about seven or eight years old."

Kaitlyn set down her tea cup and glanced toward him then back to Tillie. "They're coming to Castle Hill for a field trip?"

"Aye." Tillie gave Kaitlyn a soft smile. "And, Kaitlyn, ye'll be the perfect one to escort them."

"Don't worry." Kaitlyn served herself a sandwich. "I've heard you give the tour enough times that I can take care of it." She paused for a moment, wrinkling her nose. "The only thing is my accent. Nobody wants to listen to an American telling about a historic Irish manor."

"They'll not be lookin' for an authentic tourist experience." Tillie waved her fingers in the air. "A bit

39

o' history and a chance to spend time in the country 'tis all they're after."

"They'd be crazy not to love hearin' how ye talk," said Connor, and without waiting to see her reaction, he turned to Tillie. "The two of us will be glad to show them the manor."

Kaitlyn darted a sharp look at him, then watched her fingers running over the delicate handle of her cup. "I'd love to, Aunt Tillie, but I think I can handle it by myself..." She glanced at him again before turning back to Tillie. "I'm sure Connor has other things to do."

"I'd be pleased to help ye, Katie." He felt ridiculous at the clamminess in his palms as he waited for her to accept his offer. But they needed an opportunity to talk.

Kaitlyn didn't acknowledge him, but she continued to talk to Tillie. "I'd like to read up a bit about the manor before the children get here. Maybe find some new stories to keep their interest. Do you have a book I can borrow?"

"Aye. Ye'll be findin' all the books ye need in the library." Tillie nodded. "Connor should know where they'll be."

"Sure, and I'll take ye straight away," he said, relieved they'd finally have a chance to talk.

"I know how to find the library. Thanks." Kaitlyn dabbed her mouth with her napkin, set it on the table, and stood.

At the same time, Connor stood. "Aye, but I'm headin' that way meself. I'll join ye."

She looked at him steadily. One brow cocked the slightest bit. "I'm not going to the library right now, Connor."

Tillie stood with them.

"'Twas a lovely tea and the perfect outing today. I thank ye both." She gave each of them a hug before bustling off to tend to some guest or other.

Surely, the woman could feel the tension, but as usual, she was still a perfect hostess.

Kaitlyn left the parlor, hurried through the Great Hall, and stepped quickly up the stairs.

Connor followed. "Katie, wait."

She paused and turned, looking toward him but not meeting his gaze. "Sorry. I need to hurry. I have to get ready for my date tonight."

He stepped onto the staircase. "With Ian?" He didn't like the hot feeling that rose in his chest when he thought of her spending time with "Captain Tennis."

Katie took a step down, so she stood only a few stairs above him. She put her hands on her hips. "Yes, if you must know. When I'm not with my aunt, I plan on spending the majority of my time in Tullybrae with Ian."

"What's the story there? Is he yer man, then?" The bitterness in his tone made him feel petty. Why should he care anyway? He reminded himself of his intention to see to her safety and assessing any threat, no more than that.

She gave a slight shrug, and her eyes narrowed. "I like being with him. It's nice to have a friend here."

"I can assure ye *his* intentions aren't so pure." Connor curled his lip.

"I'm a big girl. I can handle myself." She folded her arms.

"Aye, but ye've always been too trusting of people, and that way of thinking can get ye into trouble."

Connor placed his hand on the railing and one foot up onto the next step, leaning closer.

"Well, thank you for being so concerned, but I'm not a naïve seventeen year old anymore." She raised her eyebrows and looked him straight in the face. "Maybe *my* intentions aren't that pure, either."

Her words caught him by surprise. He knew he'd hurt her, and she was speaking in anger, but her words still made his stomach clench. Katie wasn't that type of girl. "That's not like ye." He stepped up on the next stair.

"How would you know what's *like me*, Connor Flynn?" Kaitlyn scowled.

But he saw hurt in her eyes. Again. He paused, climbing another step so their eyes were level. "Because I know ye, Katie."

She lifted her chin. "No. You *knew* me. I'm not the same person I was. And you're not the same person, either." She backed up onto the next step, her gaze settling somewhere around his chin.

"'Tis true, that. We've both changed. Yer not a young girl now, but a woman grown. As much as ye might like to think otherwise, yer still the person I knew: happy, thoughtful, patient. That, I can tell by how ye've cared for Tillie."

Kaitlyn studied him for a moment then shrugged. "That's just the kind of thing Ian would say, although *he* would actually mean it."

Connor folded his arms across his chest. "Are ye trying to make me jealous, Katie?"

"Connor, I don't think I need to worry about you being jealous." Kaitlyn lowered her eyes and spoke in a soft voice. "Not when you couldn't even bear the idea that I might still wear a necklace you gave me when we were teenagers." She turned and stepped quickly up the rest of the stairs. "I can take a hint."

His grip on the railing tightened as he climbed after her. "Will ye let me explain, then?"

Kaitlyn stood at the top of the staircase. She turned her head and watched him climb the last few steps. Looking up through her lashes, she said, "You have nothing to explain, and I don't think we have anything else to say to each other." She hunched her shoulders and hurried down the hallway.

"Ye still care for me, Katie," Connor said to her retreating back then ground his jaw, regretting the words the moment they were out of his mouth. What on earth was he trying to prove?

Her step faltered, but she didn't stop until she got to her door and quickly turned the key, letting herself inside and closing the door.

Connor followed, walking into his own room, two doors farther down the hall. He sat on one of the plush leather chairs next to the fireplace. The feelings he had held in check all day came roaring to the forefront now that he was alone. Although most of the time he had successfully repressed them, his emotions regarding Katie Donovan were a tangled mass of uncertainty.

He'd felt a pull to her since they met as teenagers all those years ago, and seeing her again had just made the desire to be with her stronger. As time passed, he managed to find ways to distract himself from thinking about her. Throwing himself into his work or even spending time with other women helped for a while, but she was always there, in the back of his mind. The ache of not being with her had become so bleedin' familiar he practically didn't notice it anymore.

Tillie was right. Nothing was stronger than the pain of being apart from the one ye love. Instead of risking being hurt again, he allowed himself to become bitter and jaded.

He guarded his heart carefully, refusing to allow anyone close and not allowing them to affect him. Regarding relationships, he made sure he had complete control over his emotions. That was until he saw Katie today. Every gesture and expression she made was as familiar as if she'd never left. The confusing jumble of feelings hit him all over again. Did he still love her? The idea terrified him, but it scared him more to think that she'd gotten over him so easily when he couldn't do it himself. He stood and paced to the window.

Connor had originally come to Tullybrae with two objectives—to reclaim the necklace, and protect Katie and Tillie. But once he'd discovered Katie was unmarried, and he realized how strongly he still felt about her, his objective had shifted, and he was having trouble focusing on his original purpose.

She would leave for Seattle in a month, and he would stay in Ireland. Was exploring his feelings for Katie again worth the effort, if only for a short time? Of course not, only heartache lurked ahead. They'd tried the long-distance relationship as teenagers, and it hadn't worked out, although planning their life together through phone calls and e-mails had been nice, for a time. For more than a year, he'd done nothing but attend school and work hard with one goal in mind— making a future for the two of them.

However, as time had gone on, and he'd undertaken longer and more dangerous missions, he'd realized the wife of an agent was no life for his Katie. Their correspondence grew farther and farther apart, and finally he'd made the agonizing decision to end the relationship all together—though that choice hadn't stopped him from checking on her from time to time.

He'd casually ask Tillie about Katie's family or search for pictures of her on the internet. But, even that habit had ended when he'd seen a picture of her and her fiancé, and he couldn't bear to see any more. With that announcement, the smallest reminder of what they'd meant to each other had been smothered.

He wondered what had happened. Had the marriage not worked out? Had Katie gotten cold feet? Had that *eejit* hurt her? His jaw hurt from his clenching it. As much as he hated to imagine Katie being with another man, the thought of someone causing her any pain made Connor want to break something.

But, he only had to look at what he himself had done. He'd caused her nothing but pain. Then, and again today. Although taking the relic had undoubtedly hurt her, he told himself he had done the right thing. A small knot of guilt squirmed in Connor's stomach, but he ignored it. The relationship was better this way. Now that she no longer had the pendant, he could rest easy. He fished the necklace out of his pocket and ran his finger over the golden design, wondering how often Katie's finger had traced the very same pattern.

His mind wandered back to the night eight years ago, something he hadn't allowed himself to think about for a long time. The evening before Katie had left to return to the States, Connor gave her the pendant and explained the significance of a Celtic love knot. No beginning or end, he'd told her. The symbol represented eternity, and the love they had was eternal.

The adult Connor smiled wryly and shook his head, thinking about the sentiment. He'd been so earnest and lovesick. But he remembered how he'd felt that night. In his innocence, he believed as long as they loved each other, everything would work out. He'd held her as she cried on his shoulder, promising her someday they'd be together. Seeing the same pain on her face today and knowing this time he was the reason caused a sting in his chest.

He shook his head. He should never have given her the necklace in the first place. But at the time, he hadn't seen any harm in doing so. At least three years had passed since Seamus mentioned anything about the relics, and Connor let his teenage heart dictate his actions instead of his brain. But the problem was solved now, though not as compassionately as he'd have liked. He'd accomplished his first objective and turned his thoughts to the second. Now that he had the pendant and maintained a constant surveillance on the property, he would make sure Katie and Tillie were no longer in danger.

As he thought about Ian standing next to her and the way he'd touched her face, Connor scowled. That opponent would have to be handled differently, but he would deal with him as he would any other. Above all, he'd make sure Katie, *his* Katie, was safe.

Chapter 6

Later that evening, Connor sat at the desk in his room, his attention alternating between studying the information on his laptop and glancing out the window that overlooked the manor drive. He told himself he was just staying alert and maintaining necessary security measures at the Manor House. But if he was honest, he'd admit he was also waiting for Ian to arrive for Kaitlyn. Partly because his coming was a matter of security, but that wasn't the complete reason for his vigilance.

He looked back at the computer screen and read over the background information he'd collected about Ian Kerry. As far as Connor could tell, the man was clean. He possessed no criminal record and no known association with any suspicious groups or people. He'd gone to a private school in Belfast, attended college on a tennis scholarship, and worked at Castle Hill Manor for the last two months. Ian was apparently both a model citizen and a model employee.

Connor closed his laptop and rubbed his jaw, his shoulders tense. He'd really wanted to find something. Some reason to convince Katie to avoid Ian. He'd wanted to believe his suspicion was a gut thing instead of a jealousy thing, and he'd gotten a vibe from the guy warning him that he was dangerous.

As Connor watched out the window, an older

model blue car turned through the gate and made its way up the long drive toward the Manor House. He didn't recognize it as belonging to anyone from Tullybrae. The automobile obviously wasn't a rental car or a cab, which were the typical vehicles for a tourist. The driver was either Ian or someone else needing to be looked into. He hurried through his door just as Katie stepped out of her room.

She glanced at him before checking the handle once to make sure it was locked and turned to walk past him down the hall. She walked with her head in the air and did not look back.

"Ye'll be headin' out with Ian, then?" Connor fell into step beside her.

"Yep." Katie wore jeans and carried a sweatshirt over her arm.

Not exactly romantic dinner attire. A sigh of relief swept through his thoughts. "And where is it he'll be takin' ye?"

Katie kept walking. She waved a greeting over the railing to Ian who had just stepped through the front doors into the great hall. "Connor, what are you doing?" she whispered, not looking at him.

"Lookin' out for ye is all."

As she walked down the steps, she ran her hand along the railing, speaking out of the side of her mouth. "Whatever this is, whatever you're doing, just stop it."

"If ye'll not tell me, I'll be asking Tennis Boy."

Her neck flushed pink. "You can't have it both ways. You can't treat me the way you did, and then expect me to let you into my private life. Please just leave me alone."

"Don't be sayin' I didn't warn ye, then." Connor

strode across the great hall to where Ian stood, feeling, rather than seeing Katie hurrying to keep up. He drew near to the man. "If it isn't Mr. Ian Kerry."

Ian's eyes narrowed as he looked back and forth between the two.

Kaitlyn stepped away from Connor and to Ian's side, slipping her arm through his.

Connor's jaw clenched when Ian smugly raised his eyebrows.

"Should we get going?" Kaitlyn asked.

The smile she gave Ian was so sweet it made Connor's teeth ache. He lifted his chin, so he looked down at Ian. He put his hands in his pockets, rocking back on his heels, and spoke in a falsely friendly voice. "Where is it yer off to this evenin'?"

Ian's gaze moved to Kaitlyn and then back to Connor. His lips pursed, and his brows moved together slightly.

He was obviously deciding whether to tell Connor to mind his own business, or to brag about the date he had planned, and the fact Katie held onto *his* arm and not Connor's. The look of confusion on Ian's face was extremely satisfying.

"The caves. I'd planned on takin' Kaitlyn for a picnic, if ye'd be knowin'."

Connor could tell Ian weighed his words cautiously. Ian needed to be careful with what he said. He was dating his boss's niece, competing with her foster son, and the way he squinted and chose his words with care showed he didn't understand the dynamic between them. This scenario gave Connor the upper hand…and he knew how to use it to his advantage. "I'll be warnin' ye, Katie isn't one for high places. Don't be pressin' her to walk close to anywhere she'll be lookin' over an edge." He spoke to Ian but steadily held Katie's gaze, watching her cheeks fill with color and her mouth open slightly. "If ye've packed olives or shortbread in that picnic of yers, ye might as well be givin' them all to her now. They're her favorites, they are, and she'll not be wantin' to share."

Katie frowned as she looked between them a few times. "Ian has no problem sharing or making sure I'm safe. And more importantly, *he* treats me like an adult." She pulled on Ian's arm, stepping toward the door. "Good night, Connor," she said firmly.

He heard the slightest tremble in her voice.

"And I'll be thankin' ye for yer advice." Ian nodded.

The man's flat expression was completely at odds with his polite words. Connor followed them outside, standing on the steps and watching as Ian let Katie into his car. He shoved his hands in his pockets, leaning against the doorframe, looking casual while inside he seethed. He thought over his combat training, taking small comfort in the knowledge he was proficient in an infinite number of ways to cause Ian Kerry physical pain. But his jaw clenched when he realized as far as causing pain, Ian had the advantage without even trying.

Once they drove away, he pulled out his phone. "Aye, they're just leavin' the property now. A manky blue hatch-back. I'll be expectin' a report every half hour. I thank ye again, Matthew." Connor slid the phone back into his pocket. While he hadn't been at the agency long enough to have much seniority, plenty of agents had less. Not to mention, he had a lot of pull with his boss, Jack. Clean report or not, Connor wasn't about to trust Katie with anyone, especially when that person looked at her the way a wolf looks at a leg of mutton.

Connor spent the time she was gone eating supper with Tillie, poring over police reports, and checking his texts every half hour for Matthew's reports. He forced himself to focus on anything besides the fact that except for a junior agent following them, she had virtually no protection. On top of that, Katie was with another man, which did nothing to calm Connor's anxiety.

Five torturous hours after they'd left, Connor watched from his window as Ian's battered blue car drove slowly up the drive. He saw Ian open Katie's door and breathed a sigh of relief. *It's a wonder she's still alive after riding in that death trap.* The two spoke briefly before Katie entered the manor house alone.

His shoulders relaxed, and he rubbed the back of his neck, bending his head from side to side. He hadn't realized how tense he'd been all evening—waiting for Matthew's reports, hoping Katie was alright, and praying the tennis-playing plonker kept his hands to himself.

He listened for the sound of her bedroom door, and once he was sure she was safely inside, he stepped out of his room and walked down the familiar hallway. Although the manor was just a few hours away from his apartment, Connor had only made the trip a few times a year since he'd graduated from the Academy. His work kept him out of the country for months at a time.

The hallway windows looked out on the darkening countryside. The hour was past ten, and the long summer day was nearly in darkness. He paused, while bits of memory from his childhood surfaced—Hide and Seek in the manicured grounds, riding his bicycle home from school in Tullybrae, exploring the hills beyond the manor property. Memories filled him with warm nostalgia. For as long as he should live, Connor would always consider the manor house home.

Lost in thought, he continued down the hall and stepped across the threshold of the library. His throat constricted as he glanced toward Seamus's favorite wing-back chair next to the fireplace. Seamus had sat here nearly every evening, reading or chatting with guests.

Connor walked to the worn chair, placing his hand on the armrest where Seamus's elbow rubbed the tapestry fabric thin. Then he sat and leaned back his head. The memories came in a flood now, and Connor pressed his palms against his eyes. He thought of all the times they spent together in this room.

When Connor was a boy, Seamus patiently helped him with his schoolwork at the desk. Then later as a man, they sat next to each other, reading or talking over a glass of brandy in the evening. Seamus was the only father Connor ever knew. Seamus commanded respect, and Connor worked every day to make him proud. He even followed in the older man's footsteps, training at the Academy and joining G2. Seeing the satisfaction in Seamus's face when he graduated with honors and was accepted into the Agency had been one of the greatest moments of Connor's life. An ache grew in his chest.

Connor prided himself on the ability to remain objective about most things. So, he wasn't prepared for the shock of having his emotions take over. Seamus'ss loss nearly overwhelmed him. His heart hurt, and he leaned forward with his elbows on his knees and rubbed his fingers into his eyes. *Dammit, Seamus. Why hadn't ye told me yer concerns sooner?* Could Connor have prevented his death? He should have been here two weeks earlier to take care of Tillie. Why hadn't he visited more often?

He had so much he wished he'd told Seamus. Did Seamus even know how much Connor admired him? Appreciated him? Loved him? Guilt and sorrow gnawed at his chest. He hadn't felt a loss this deeply since his own mother had died over twenty years ago. Not having better control of his feelings frustrated him.

Jennifer Moore

Chapter 7

Kaitlyn lay in bed, snuggled beneath a soft quilt, but for the life of her, she couldn't wind down. She squeezed her hands into fists, still livid when she thought about her day with Mr. Connor Flynn. Not only had he completely humiliated her at the cemetery, a few hours later he did it again with his little alpha-male stunt. The thought of his arrogant face as he spoke to Ian infuriated her. Connor acted like he knew Kaitlyn inside and out, and he was letting Ian spend time with *his* woman. To calm herself, she took slow, deep breaths.

Connor's interference made their date uncomfortable and awkward, and they couldn't quite return to their easy friendly companionship. And in addition, Kaitlyn couldn't get the things Connor said out of her mind. Why did he remember those details? Had he just stored up little bits of trivia to torture her? And why did she feel a little flattered he had remembered her personality quirks? She was so frustrated and confused regarding that man.

Just for a moment at the cemetery, when she'd sat by him, she saw the familiar look in his eyes that set her heart racing. The look she'd thought he'd reserved just for her, and when she did, she felt something between them that was warm and electric and amazing. She thought Connor had felt it, too. The things she felt had been real, hadn't they? But obviously they were only real for her. And that realization made her whole toe-curling humiliation even worse, because she'd let herself hope.

Pulling on a robe over her pajamas, she walked down the hall to the library. She'd been so upset earlier thanks to Connor and worried she would run into him in the library that she hadn't even done the research for the field trip tomorrow. When she stepped into the room, she froze mid-step.

Connor sat in Uncle Seamus's favorite chair near the fireplace, his head in his hands.

Guilt squirmed in Kaitlyn's stomach. She'd spent so much time being angry at Connor and worried about her own feelings, she hadn't even thought about how he must be grieving. She walked closer, kneeling on the carpet beside him. Gently, she laid a hand on his arm and felt him start. "I'm sorry about Seamus, Connor."

He rubbed his eyes then he raised his head.

His look of pain and vulnerability pierced her. How could she be so angry at this man? Kaitlyn continued softly, "The two of you had a special relationship, and I know how hard it is to lose someone you love and admire."

Connor lifted her hand off his arm. He held it in both of his, studying it. "I thank ye, Katie. I'm needin' to apologize for the way I've treated ye since arrivin' this mornin'. Truly, 'twasn't my intention to hurt ye." He looked up.

Kaitlyn's breath caught in her throat.

"But, circumstances exist that I can't explain to ye now. Things ye don't understand. I'm tryin' to protect ye, is all."

"Well, how very chivalrous." Kaitlyn's body tensed. She pulled away her hand and stood. "I'm so glad you're *protecting* me from something as threatening as a necklace and a tennis player who wants to date me. I don't know how you sleep at night with this kind of peril on your doorstep." She pressed her hands on her hips, looking toward the bookcases lining the walls of the library. "Can you just show me where to find the book I asked Aunt Tillie for? Then I'll retreat to the safety of my bedroom before I'm tempted to do anything as dangerous as wearing jewelry or having a picnic again."

For several seconds, Connor didn't say anything. He studied her, scratching his cheek.

Kaitlyn crossed her arms and waited.

"And what do ye think Ian's intentions are toward ye?"

So, now he's taking on the role of big brother. She lifted her chin. "I really don't think that's any of your business."

"I told ye, I'm just watchin' out for ye, Katie."

She shifted, putting her hands on her hips. "Well, whether that's true or not, I don't need anyone to watch out for me. I'm a big girl, and I'm stronger than I seem." She looked away from his steady gaze. "I've handled a lot by myself."

"But true as I'm tellin' ye, some things ye still need protectin' from. I know ye've been strong. Through yer ma's death and yer broken engagement."

Kaitlyn's gaze snapped back to his, and her last bit of confidence crumbled. Her stomach burned. "How do you know about that?" she said, her voice cracking. "Aunt Tillie wouldn't have…"

Connor squinted, and his nose wrinkled slightly.

Any other time she would have thought he looked like an adorably penitent schoolboy. But she had no such kind thoughts about him right now.

"Tillie didn't betray yer confidence." He tilted his head to the side and leaned toward her. "What happened, Katie? Did he—"

Kaitlyn's heart had been strained past its breaking point. The ache wasn't easing, and every interaction with Connor was just hurting it further. Asking about her broken engagement on the same day he'd rejected, embarrassed, and lied was so humiliating, the entire situation was nearly comical. Nearly.

Even though almost a year had passed since she'd called off the engagement, remembering how hurt Todd looked was still painful as was remembering how lonely she'd felt afterwards. Kaitlyn had done the right thing, but that didn't mean forgetting the future they'd planned together and continuing on with her life alone had been easy.

"What happened is he got tired of waiting for me to fall in love with him, and I got tired of trying." Exhaustion swamped her body and she slumped. She couldn't meet Connor's gaze and turned toward the fire. She heard him walk to a shelf and glanced up to see him sliding out a large book along with a few small ones. Seeing him extend the volumes, she grabbed them to her chest and turned to make her getaway.

"Katie."

She stopped partway through the door, dreading what he might say.

"I thank ye for yer condolences tonight."

"You're welcome," she said in a small voice, still

unable to meet his gaze and moved to leave.

"And, Katie…"

This time, she turned, connecting with his gaze. Connor's eyes were soft.

"He's a fool. Yer worth waitin' for."

She hurried away, her confused feelings at war with one another. Did Connor mean what he'd said? Could she trust him? If the answer was yes, did she dare?

Chapter 8

The next morning, Kaitlyn paced over the plank flooring in her room, her new tennis skirt moving against her legs. Aunt Tillie would be expecting her for breakfast, but she dreaded the idea of running into Connor again. The last thing she wanted was another uncomfortable encounter.

She walked into the bathroom and checked her hair, again. Was it better to go down earlier and hope he'd sleep in? Or should she wait until later and hope he'd already eaten? The idea of seeing him made her stomach tighten, and frustration fueled her moves because a little part of her hoped he would be waiting, her heart even tripped a little at the thought. Her heart obviously needed a refresher course on not opening itself to being hurt again.

Yesterday had been one big mess of humiliation and confusion. Not to mention she'd been replaying constantly in her mind the words Connor spoke as she left the library. Why did he say things like that? Just to mess with her? She didn't think she could handle spending more time with him. Not with her emotions so raw. Especially when he'd been clear he wasn't actually interested in her. She squeezed lotion onto her hands, rubbing it onto her bare shoulders as she moved back to the bedroom.

She couldn't very well avoid Connor the entire

time she was in Ireland, either. Besides, hunger attacked her stomach, Aunt Tillie waited, and Ian would appear in an hour for her tennis lesson. So, her choices were either the possibility of facing Connor at breakfast now, or being hungry until lunch. She might as well just bite the bullet and go downstairs.

Kaitlyn put on earrings, and out of habit, she reached for her necklace. The entire horrible scene came back with nauseating clarity when she remembered why it wasn't sitting on her dresser. This fact only firmed up her resolve to guard her feelings when Connor was around. She took a deep breath and let it out before stepping into the hall, glancing at Connor's closed door, and then she hurried down the stairs.

She walked into the inn's dining room—a banquet hall with elaborately carved wooden beams and heavy iron chandeliers. She made her way through the white linen-covered tables set with sparkling china, smiling at a few of the other guests she'd met during her visit. She sat at her regular table next to Aunt Tillie who wrote in neat cursive in her notebook. "Good morning." She leaned over to give her aunt a one-armed hug.

"And a lovely day 'tis, now that ye're here, Kaitlyn." Tillie nodded toward a server, waving her over. "Are ye ready for breakfast?"

"Morning to ye, ma'am." The girl bobbed her head and bounced in a small curtsey. "And to ye, Miss Kaitlyn."

"Hi, Darcy." Kaitlyn smiled at the young woman's splash of freckles.

"I'm ready for my usual breakfast, now, if ye please." Tillie closed her notebook and set the pen neatly beside it.

"Of course, ma'am." Darcy bobbed again. "And for ye, Miss Kaitlyn?"

"I'd like some porridge, please." Kaitlyn couldn't help but smile every time she said the word. When she ordered "porridge," she felt like Goldilocks, but she'd discovered ordering "oatmeal" only produced blank stares from the servers.

Darcy placed one hand on her hip and wagged her finger. "If ye don't mind me sayin', Miss Kaitlyn, ye'll be needin' more than just porridge, or ye'll waste away quick as a wink."

Kaitlyn smiled. "I don't think anyone is in danger of wasting away with all the good food at Castle Hill Manor. Porridge will be plenty. Thanks, Darcy."

"As ye like, then." Darcy headed back to the kitchen, but she paused mid-turn and froze for an instant before regaining her composure and bustling off to the kitchen.

Kaitlyn looked up, wondering what had startled her and saw Connor walking across the room toward them. *Of course. Who else has the power to stop a woman in her tracks?* She made a point of *not* looking at him and *not* noticing he wore a blue button-down shirt that emphasized his broad shoulders, stretched around his biceps, and made his eyes even more vibrant—if that was possible. She turned toward Aunt Tillie. "What's on the schedule for today?"

"Oh, 'tis a busy day, for sure. Glad I am to have yer–" Tillie glanced up. "Oh, good mornin' to ye, Connor."

There's another woman under his spell.

Connor walked to their table. *"Dia dhuit ar*

maidin." He leaned between them to kiss Tillie on the cheek.

Kaitlyn leaned away, ignoring his spicy smell.

"*Móra na maidine dhuit.*" Tillie indicated the chair next to Kaitlyn and motioned toward the server who hurried back toward them. "Have a seat then, my dear. Darcy, please bring Connor a full breakfast."

"I thank ye, Darcy." Connor gave a smile.

Kaitlyn tried not to roll her eyes when the woman's light complexion turned beet red.

"Good mornin', Katie," he said.

"Morning." Kaitlyn kept her voice light and turned back to Tillie. "You were just telling me about your busy day, weren't you, Aunt Tillie?"

"Aye, apparently, I'll be needin' to meet with the *guarda* as well as Seamus'ss lawyer." Tillie's brows pulled together.

Connor tensed, and his eyes squinted as he watched Tillie. "And do ye know what it's about, then?"

"I've no idea, though I've been assured 'tis all regular procedure."

"Do you need someone to go with you?" Kaitlyn asked. "I'm sure—"

"*Nil*, I'd much rather ye and Connor tend to the manor and the tour," she said.

Darcy, who had apparently found a moment in the kitchen to apply fresh lip gloss, arrived with breakfast.

She set their meals in front of them and spent extra time fussing over Connor's plate. "And is there anythin' else ye'll be needin'?" she asked, shaking her dark curls slightly.

"I thank ye. This'll be fine," said Tillie.

Darcy bobbed one last time and left them to their

meal.

Connor spread his napkin over his lap before turning to Tillie. "Yer sure?"

As she poured coffee for the three of them, Tillie nodded.

Connor was quiet for a moment. He reached forward and picked up a coffee cup, setting it beside his plate. "What time will the snappers be arriving, then?"

"Half past ten."

"Perfect. 'Twill give me time to finish a bit o' work I'm needin' to have done this mornin'." He took a sip of coffee. "Have we a count o' how many we should be plannin' on?"

"No more than twenty," Tillie poured cream into her cup. "Sure and Kaitlyn'll be glad for yer help."

"I can really handle the visit by myself." She was being rude, but the last thing she wanted was to spend the entire day sorting out the confusion of feelings Connor created.

"Course ye can, darlin'." Tillie sipped her drink. "But 'twill do ye both good to work together."

Connor wiped his napkin across his mouth. "I'd feel better bein' close, makin' sure ye were protected."

Kaitlyn looked at the ceiling, letting out a breath, and shaking her head. She was getting tired of him being so controlling. Besides, Tillie needed him more than she did right now. "Connor, I can manage a group of kids on my own. It's what I do every single day at work. If one of them turns out to be a ninja assassin or something, I'll call you." She plunged her spoon into her porridge a bit too hard. She turned toward him and forced an even tone into her words. "Will you please stop treating me like a child?"

Connor held her gaze with his own. He leaned close. "No man with eyes in his head would be mistakin' ye for a child, Katie."

His low tone made her thoughts scatter. As much as she tried not to, Kaitlyn was the first to look away. Her cheeks burned, and her pulse pounded in her ears.

For a few minutes, they ate silently. Kaitlyn shoved aside the feelings Connor's words aroused. Did he have to do this? One minute he acted like she was a helpless infant that needed constant protection, and then the next, he said something with his woman-killing smolder that made her brain forget all its resolve before he'd walked in the room. All of his charm was an act. He didn't care for her, hadn't contacted her in eight years, and the necklace…

Pouring buttermilk and sugar on her porridge, she concentrated on her breakfast. She loved how thick and chewy it was and was glad Aunt Tillie convinced her to try it the "authentic Irish" way.

Connor shifted, and his leg brushed hers under the table.

Based on the way she jumped, Kaitlyn might as well have received an electric shock from his touch. She crossed her legs and angled them toward Aunt Tillie, wishing the chairs had been placed farther apart on the round table. The nerves on the side of her body facing him were hyper-sensitive, and every time he came close to touching her again, she felt goose bumps rise on her skin. "Well, it's time for my lesson," she said, standing.

At the same time, Connor stood.

Kaitlyn gave Aunt Tillie a quick hug. "Good luck today, and if you need to take Connor to your meeting,

I'll be fine on my own." She avoided looking toward Connor.

Why couldn't her feelings about this man be straightforward and uncomplicated? She walked through the tables, unwilling to acknowledge the burning feel of Connor's gaze.

****

Connor watched Katie walk through the dining room doors, reeling from the cold way she acted. *And why shouldn't she?*

He needed a chance to explain himself and to repair things. To start over. And she deserved an explanation. At the cemetery, he'd been more concerned with her safety than with explaining why she couldn't wear the necklace, and he'd ended up hurting her. Worse, he hadn't told her why he had broken off contact years ago—that reason was something he didn't fully understand himself. Unfortunately, the result was, in Katie's eyes, he'd ended up looking like the world's biggest arse.

"Time's all she's needin'." Tillie reached across the empty seat to grasp Connor's hand.

Lost in thought, he hadn't realized he was still staring at the doorway. "'Twill take more than time to fix the *hames* I've made with Katie."

"Nonsense. 'Tis an old lady I am, but still I'm seein' the way yer face softens when ye look at our Kaitlyn, and the way she'll look at ye when she thinks nobody's watchin'. I'm not knowin' what happened all these years ago, but I do see something special exists between the two of ye."

Though her words were meant to inspire hope, he didn't feel it. "I'm afraid Katie's not seein' it. Not anymore."

"'Tis as I said, give her time. I know 'tisn't yer strongest quality, but ye'll do well to be patient."

"All the patience in the world 'twon't be enough to fix everythin' I've banjaxed with Katie."

Tillie pursed her lips and tilted her head at Connor. "With yer patience then, ye might be needin' to add a bit o' charm. And *that* 'tis somethin' I know ye can do."

Connor lifted Tillie's hand and pressed a kiss on it. He wished more than anything that he had the same faith in himself that Tillie had in him. If he did repair the relationship, what then? Could he bear to lose Katie again?

Chapter 9

Two hours later, Connor paced his room, his hand tight on the phone at his ear. "Apparently, the local *guarda* have called in Tillie, Jack. What have ye found?"

"Nothin' conclusive, I'm afraid. They'll just be askin' her about Seamus's habits, had he been feelin' well that day, and things like that."

"Weeks later?" Questioning a family member this long after the crime was outside normal procedures.

"Aye, we're graspin' at straws here. Without exhuming the body, we've only a few blood samples to work with. More tests are needed yet."

"Ye'll tell me when ye know somethin' for sure, then." Connor stopped pacing to look out the window at the bus pulling through the gates.

"That I will, Connor. And how's yer country vacation goin'?"

He rubbed his eyes. "I'm to mind a group of High Babies this mornin'."

Jack barked a laugh. "'Tis somethin' I'd be payin' to see, for my imagination isna able to produce such an image. Connor Flynn with a pack o' *chisselers*. Aye, that Tillie has a grand sense of humor." He laughed again. "And I wish ye luck, man, though I'll wager 'tis the wee *gasún* who'll be needin it."

Connor ended the call and pushed the phone into

his pocket as he walked through the front doors and down the manor house steps.

The bus doors opened, and the children bounded out, screaming and running and generally causing chaos.

Katie stood next to the bus, talking to an elderly white-haired woman who Connor assumed was the school teacher. Connor noticed Katie now wore slacks and a fitted blouse. The thick belt she wore over the blouse pulled in at her small waist and gave her a perfect hourglass figure.

As he walked closer, he continued to admire her, but the moment was short lived as he had to fight to keep his balance when a group of boys nearly ran him down, yelling and tumbling over each other like puppies. He had little experience with children. And for very good reason. They were loud, sticky, and uncontrollable, and his forehead prickled, indicating an oncoming headache.

By the time he got to where the frazzled teacher was calling for the children's attention, Katie was already in the middle of the group. As he watched her talking to a few of them, he noticed something happening. She led them in a game that involved soft talk and taps to different places on her face and arms. And with each round, more children noticed and joined in. The volume of the chaos reduced.

Connor took a few steps closer until he could hear what she said.

"If you can hear me," Katie spoke in a soft voice. "Touch your nose…"

The children all touched their noses and crowded closer, listening.

"If you can hear me, clap your hands…"

The children clapped. By this time, they were all gathered around her.

"If you can hear me, fold your arms…"

The entire group folded their arms as one.

Astonishment filled him at the way she had taken control of the situation, and instead of yelling or threatening, she used her gentle nature to calm the children.

"Now, that's better," Kaitlyn said with a nod. "I'd like to welcome you to Castle Hill Manor. My name is Miss Donovan, and my helper over there is Mr. Flynn." She waved in Connor's direction.

He smiled uncertainly as the children turned toward him.

Kaitlyn started speaking in her gentle voice again, recapturing their attention. "I know the bus ride was long, and you all have wiggles to get out, but before we do anything else, you need to know the rules, all right?" She waited until she had every child's attention. "The first rule is, we need to stay together as a group. Who should you ask if you need to use the bathroom? Or if—" She stopped talking as a few of the children giggled.

Seeing the look of confusion on her face, Connor cleared his throat. "I think Miss Donovan means if ye need to use the *toilet*."

Kaitlyn smiled before she continued. "If you need to use the toilet, who should you ask?"

A boy raised his hand.

Kaitlyn nodded. "Do you know the answer?"

"We ask ye or him or Mrs. Flanagan." He pointed at each adult in turn.

"Excellent," Kaitlyn said. "And what is your name?"

"Dylan."

"Everybody, Dylan has perfectly demonstrated the next rule. The Manor House is a special place, and while we're inside, we need to act politely and not interrupt when someone else is speaking. If you have a question for me or Mr. Flynn or Mrs. Flanagan, you must raise your hand instead of shouting. Thank you, Dylan."

The boy beamed at her praise.

A small wiggle of envy moved in Connor's chest. Was he really jealous of a little kid?

Kaitlyn opened her mouth to say something else when she saw one of the girls had a hand raised. "Yes?"

"And why do ye speak strange-like?"

"That question is a very good one." Kaitlyn held out her hand. "Will you tell me your name?"

"Sorcha."

"Sorcha, the reason why I sound different than all of you is because I am from the United States. This is how we talk. One of my favorite things about coming to Ireland is hearing how all of *you* speak. I love the accent because it sounds beautiful and musical."

Again, Sorcha raised her hand.

"Yes, Sorcha?"

"'Tis normal how we talk."

She looked around the group, including the others in the conversation. "Yes, isn't that interesting how it sounds normal to you, and the way I speak sounds normal to me, but we can still understand each other, can't we?"

A dark-haired boy raised his hand.

She nodded toward him. "What's your question?"

Connor wondered how she could possibly be so patient with the children's constant interruptions.

"I think 'tis grand how ye speak."

She leaned forward, holding out her hand toward the boy. "What's your name?"

"Sean."

"Thank you, Sean. I like how you talk, too."

Another boy's hand shot into the air.

"Yes?"

"Patrick's me name. And y'are fierce lovely."

A smile lit up Katie's face.

The sight made Connor's heart leap. She pressed her lips tight, highlighting her dimples. He'd forgotten about her dimples, and sullenness coated his thoughts. He wished he'd been the one to cause her smile.

"Thank you, Patrick. What a nice thing to say." Her eyes shone. "Well, before we go inside the manor house, I'd like to see if you know what a manor house was used for? What kind of people used to live here?"

Kaitlyn patiently listened to each of the children's answers before she continued. "A manor house is where the lord of the manor lived. Here in Tullybrae, Lord O'Brien was in charge of making sure everybody obeyed the laws. His job was to keep the people safe from invaders. He let people have farms on his land and live in his village, but they had to pay him. Sometimes, they paid him with food from their farms or by helping take care of the manor. And sometimes, they paid with money." She scanned the crowd and took a breath.

"I want you to turn around and look." Kaitlyn swept her hands, indicating the green hills and forests surrounding them. "Long ago, a lord ruled Castle Hill

Manor, and everything you can see belonged to him."

A girl with red braids raised her hand.

"Yes?" Katie acknowledged her.

"'Tisn't fair."

"Hm…it doesn't seem fair now, does it?" Katie nodded. "But whether everyone was treated fairly depended on the lord of the manor. Sometimes, the lord was kind, and he took care of all the people who lived on his lands. He made sure they had enough crops, and if a problem arose, people would come to him, and he would help them. He didn't want any of his people to be hungry or unhappy."

She moved a few feet in each direction, keeping their attention as she spoke. "But, sometimes the lord wasn't kind. And he liked to have other people do all the work for him. Let's walk inside, and I'll tell you a story about a lord of the manor who wasn't very nice to his people. And what happened to him." Kaitlyn led the group through the main doors.

When he saw the wide-eyes as the children stepped through the doors and into the great hall, Connor smiled. He'd been inside the entry hall so often that sometimes he forgot how impressive it was.

The children craned their necks, looking up at the high ceilings. Huge fireplaces with carved wooden mantles stood at either end of the hall. Swords and coats of arms hung above them, but by far, the statue of Angus O'Brien dominated the space and overshadowed everything else. The group stopped in front of the statue.

As they looked at the lord's scowling face, a few children pursed their lips, looking upward with creased brows. Angus certainly didn't have a welcoming aspect.

"Here we are," Kaitlyn spread her arm in a grand gesture. "This statute is Lord Angus O'Brien." She paused until she had every child's attention before she continued talking. "Remember how I told you that some lords weren't very nice? Well, he was one of the most selfish of all. Lord Angus made the people pay so much money to live on his land that many of his subjects didn't have enough food for their families. He didn't protect the farms from wild animals or thieves, and the people were hungry and afraid.

"Lord Angus had a scary face that always scowled, and he had a terrible accident, which left him walking with a limp. The people called him a beast, because he was so cruel and looked so wicked. The legend says that Lord Angus had a secret treasure—"

Connor's stomach plummeted. What was she doing? "Kat—Miss Donovan, do ye think ye should be tellin' this story, it…'tisn't in the usual tour—"

All of the children turned.

Katie stared. Her pinched brows were quickly replaced by narrowed eyes and a clenched jaw. She folded her arms. "Mr. Flynn. I need to remind you of the rule about interrupting when somebody else is speaking."

A few of the children giggled.

"Aye, but the story, 'tis—"

"Thank you, Mr. Flynn." Katie raised and lowered her eyebrows quickly. She looked back at the children who had been watching the exchange closely. "Where was I?"

Should he stop her? Make a scene? Connor took a few steps toward her, but she shot him a look that stopped him in his tracks. He didn't know how to proceed. He looked around, grateful no one else was near enough to hear. Seamus gave him the impression that the story of Angus's treasure was a family secret.

Kaitlyn took a breath. "Stories were told of Lord Angus having a hidden treasure. So, many of his hungry people would sneak into the manor, or onto the grounds, to search for it." She frowned at Connor. "But when they were caught, Lord Angus would punish them."

Connor glanced at the children enraptured by her story. He rubbed the back of his neck, noting the headache he'd noticed earlier was building.

"One day," she continued, "Lord Angus began to feel sick. He got so sick he couldn't get out of bed, and his doctors didn't know what was wrong. After weeks of being extremely ill, he finally died. Many people believe he was poisoned, but nobody could ever prove whether or not it was true. His son, Quinn, became the next lord of the manor. Quinn O'Brien was nothing like his father. His mother had taught him to be a kind man. He was good to his people and helped make Tullybrae a happy place to live again. But, although he and all of his descendants searched, nobody ever found Lord Angus's treasure."

Connor looked up at the statue's face and then back at Katie. If she only knew how that "legend" had shaped later lives. How many people had fought and died because of the treasure. Perhaps even Seamus. He rubbed his forehead and wondered what she would think if she knew just how closely her own life was linked to the legend of Angus O'Brien.

Chapter 10

What is his deal? Really? 'I don't think ye should be telling this story'? Is Connor Flynn the most controlling and annoying person on the planet?

When Kaitlyn passed Connor, she flipped her ponytail. The action was childish, but childish was how he made her feel. She led the children through the Great Hall, smiling when she overheard many of them coming up with different theories about the treasure's location. Last night, she'd been thrilled to discover a few lines about the treasure legend in one of the journals Connor shared from the library. What a perfect story for a group of kids.

Of course, Connor had been irritated she'd strayed from Aunt Tillie's usual tour script. The man had serious control issues. Maybe he could give her just a little credit and realize she might know a thing or two about what children were interested in.

As they walked through the portrait gallery, a girl tugged on Connor's hand. He knelt so he was eye to eye with her, listened to what she said, and nodded as he answered. Then he stood and spoke to Mrs. Flanagan who walked with the girl through the door into the dining room. A few minutes later, when Mrs. Flanagan and the girl returned, the little girl walked back to Connor and slipped her hand into his.

He looked down and winked.

Kaitlyn bit back at a sigh, her heart softening. The short exchange held her mesmerized. She hadn't expected this side of Connor. In fact, he'd looked nothing but irritated and impatient with the children since they'd arrived. The warmth filling her chest as the little girl looked up at him with a trusting gaze while he spoke kindly caught her unawares. Every time she thought she had figured out Connor Flynn, he surprised her.

Once they finished the tour of the house and walked outside, Kaitlyn led all the children to a grassy area where their teacher had set out blankets and sack lunches. Kaitlyn made sure the children were all settled before she sat and chatted with some of the kids who scooted closer. They asked her about her home and giggled at words she used. She saw that a few little girls sat next to Connor. *Naturally*. He leaned back on one arm, one leg bent, and he chatted with them as they ate. The girls were obviously smitten, vying for his attention.

As the children finished eating, groups explored the grounds nearby—hiding in the tall hedges or looking at the fountains. One boy produced a soccer ball, and the grassy area instantly became a football pitch.

Mrs. Flanagan walked around, keeping an eye on the wanderers, and Kaitlyn sat with a group on a blanket they'd moved out of the way. Several of the girls played a hand-clapping, rhyming game, and they giggled at Kaitlyn's accent as she repeated the chant and learned the rhythm. She looked around, searching for where Connor had gone. Had he gotten tired of the whole thing and just left?

From the other side of the pitch, she heard children yelling, "Mr. Flynn! Mr. Flynn!" and turned toward the soccer game just in time to see Connor skillfully stop a pass and juggle the ball on his knee a few times before kicking it to a boy who waved to him. The boy passed it back. Connor ran up the field and kicked it between the rocks that marked the goal.

The children cheered.

"And is Mr. Flynn yer fella, then?"

Kaitlyn turned from the game to see Sorcha looking at her. "No." Irritation hit her with the way her cheeks heated, and the fact this girl could read her so well. "Mr. Flynn is just a friend of mine."

Sorcha watched the game. "Sure, and I wish I was his *oul-doll*." She sighed. "He's fierce handsome is Mr. Flynn."

Kaitlyn raised a brow, surprised that an eight year old would have such an opinion. She watched Connor running and calling out to the kids, rallying his team, darting to block a pass, and ruffling a boy's hair when he scored.

He looked up and smiled.

His boyish look caused her heart to trip. She had to agree with Sorcha, Mr. Flynn *was* fierce handsome.

When Mrs. Flanagan announced their departure time had come, Kaitlyn and Connor helped gather the children and stood by the bus, saying their goodbyes. They waved as the bus drove down the drive, and then walked together toward the Manor House.

Kaitlyn's mind was a whirl. Connor had been so…adorable with the kids. Her heart softened toward him, just like last night in the library. Sometimes, his cool exterior cracked just a bit, and she saw a trait inside him that she'd remembered from so long ago. A gentleness and warmth. She saw it in the way he acted toward Aunt Tillie, and then she caught glimpses today when he was with the children. Kaitlyn wished she'd been the one that brought out this kindness in him but cut off the thought before it took hold. Her stomach grew heavy. He wasn't interested in her, and she needed to get over that notion.

Aunt Tillie met them as they walked through the doors, and Kaitlyn instantly knew something was wrong. Her aunt's face was drawn, and her eyes were red like she'd been crying.

"My dears. 'Tis glad I am that yer here." She reached up to pat Connor's cheeks then she hugged Katie.

Connor placed a hand on Tillie's shoulder, and he glanced at Katie.

The look on his face mirrored the concern she felt. "Aunt Tillie, are you all right?"

"Aye, though I've matters to discuss with the two of ye. We'll take our tea on the patio, then. I'll just pop in and notify the kitchen."

Katie watched Tillie walk through the dining room doors, heading toward the kitchen. "Do you think the lawyer said something to upset her?" She chewed on her lip. "Or maybe the police?"

"Aye." Connor rubbed his chin. His brows furrowed. "Tillie's not one to overreact. If she's lookin' upset, I've no doubt 'tis for a good reason."

They walked through the dining room and out onto the patio overlooking the Manor House gardens. Kaitlyn loved the view from the patio. Flowers bloomed everywhere, exploding with color, set against the backdrop of green Ireland was so famous for.

Connor let out a breath and rolled back his shoulders. "I don't know how ye manage to do it every day. A few hours with the snappers, and I'm exhausted."

"You were great with the kids, Connor." Kaitlyn leaned her back against the wrought-iron rail that surrounded the balcony. "Also, you're a talented soccer player."

He leaned against the rail next to her. "Ye'd be hard pressed to find an Irish lad who couldna' hold his own in a football match with eight year olds." Connor placed a hand on the rail just inches from hers. "Playin' is grand, sure. But when it comes to patience and keepin' their attention, 'tis ye who's a natural."

"It's my job." Kaitlyn shrugged, her heart warming at his praise.

"I've not much experience with children."

"Don't any of your friends have kids?"

"Aye, some. But I'm in no hurry to join the poor blokes." He bumped her shoulder gently. "And what about ye, Katie? I can envision ye wantin' a house full o' wee ones someday."

"I'd love that," she said, the familiar ache rising in her heart. "I always wished I was part of a big family, but mine was just me and my parents."

"And now they're gone." He slid his hand to hers, intertwining their fingers. "Yer lonely, then."

Kaitlyn resisted the heat his touch ignited in her skin. "Not too lonely. I have friends, and when school's in session, the kids in my class kind of become my little family." She hated how defensive she sounded and how much she loved feeling his hand on hers.

"But 'tisn't a substitute for a family of yer own, is what yer thinkin'?"

"Well, of course, I'd love a family of my own, but the opportunity just…it just hasn't worked out yet." *Obviously.* Why did he have to bring up this subject again? Just to humiliate her? What was he doing? Why pretend he cared? Coldness replaced her warm contentment. She pulled her hand out of his and moved away. "What about you and your um…your *oul-doll*?" She knew she butchered the pronunciation. "I bet she'll want a family sometime, right?" The words hurt. She swallowed hard. They hurt to even think about. But she felt empowered, able to face the pain, and say it out loud.

Connor raised his brows and tilted his head to the side. "What would be givin' ye the idea I had a lady, then?"

Kaitlyn pursed her lips, feeling a little confused and a lot angry. "Because you…the necklace. I—"

He lifted his chin, a hint of a smile appearing. "Ah, ye assumed I was takin' it to give it to someone else. 'Tis no wonder ye were upset. Katie, I've no one I'd be givin' it to. I told ye the truth when I said I was keepin' ye safe."

Kaitlyn pushed away from the railing and turned to face him. "Actually, I think that explanation makes it worse. At least, thinking you wanted it for someone else was easier than knowing you just didn't want *me* to have it." She fought against allowing her voice to tremble.

Connor rubbed the back of his neck with his palm. "'Tis a long story, but if ye've a mind to listen, I'll tell ye, then. Though I'd ask ye not to repeat it, as I promised when the tale was told to me so many years ago."

She crossed her arms, resisting the urge to storm away or to run and hide. "Connor, all I know is you've been acting all kinds of strange since you got here. I'm getting mixed signals, and you seem to just be making up a crazy story to explain away your actions." Why couldn't he just be up front?

"Katie. Circumstances exist that ye just don't understand. Truly I know it sounds crazy, but I've not told ye a falsehood. I can promise, yer safety is what I'm most concerned about. If anything were to happen to ye…"

Apparently, he was determined to hold onto his story. A sudden spurt of anger rose inside, and she held it in, letting out a puff of air rather than screaming. "Oh, that's right. I *forgot*. The necklace is *dangerous*. And telling kids a legend, in *Ireland* of all places…" She spread her arms dramatically. "That's dangerous, too."

"Katie, I've a good reason for not wantin' ye to tell the story to the children."

"What reason is that?"

He stared for a long moment before he answered. "Treasure hunters. We're not wantin' to encourage treasure hunters. And so, we've kept the story a secret."

She folded her arms across her chest. His explanation almost made sense, but he'd paused too long before he'd answered. As if he was coming up with a story. She might have even believed him if not for the whole *"I took the necklace to protect you"* excuse.

How could she trust him? Why did wanting to trust him frustrate her so badly? He was charming to her and adorable with the kids one minute, then patronizing and spouting crazy talk the next. "Connor, I don't understand your weird control issues, or the game you're playing. I think you could at least grow up and do me the courtesy of telling me the truth."

Chapter 11

Connor's mind spun, thoughts tumbling over one another. How could he possibly convince Katie he had her best intentions at heart when she wouldn't even give him the chance to explain himself? Surely, she'd felt the heat when their hands touched. At times, she seemed to soften toward him, but she could throw up her defensive wall at a moment's notice. She'd obviously learned how to protect herself from being hurt. And every time he felt like they were making progress—that she was listening, and he was repairing their relationship—he said or did something stupid to ruin it.

He was more than a little relieved when Tillie walked through the doors onto the patio, and Katie went to her, putting an arm around the old woman's slight shoulders and leading her toward a table. Connor knew Tillie wouldn't start a serious conversation until they all had been served their tea, and so he held off asking the questions that were eating at him.

Tillie sat between them, folding her hands in her lap. "And tell me about the tour this mornin', then. How did it go with the High Babies?"

"They were super," Kaitlyn answered, a wide smile lighting her face. "We had a lot of fun, didn't we, Connor?"

He was relieved Katie would put aside their issues

to help Tillie. "Aye, but 'tis ye who were the favorite. Playin' games and entertainin' them with yer stories."

Katie glanced at him.

He saw the anger she'd felt a few moments ago was being slowly replaced with a blush of gratitude.

"You're the soccer hero. And you were a hit with the little girls."

"Certainly, ye had yer fair share of admirers. Patrick, was it? Proclaimin' yer beauty for all to hear." He waved a hand in the air.

"And 'tis glad I am to see the two of ye gettin' along so splendidly." Tillie looked back and forth between them with a smile.

Darcy approached and placed a tray with a tea set and finger sandwiches on the table.

"Thank ye." Tillie nodded.

The server curtsied and smiled at Connor before she walked back through the doors into the dining room.

Tillie poured the tea and passed around cups and the plate of food.

"How did the meetin' go this mornin' then?" Connor leaned forward, his voice lowered, ready to discuss the real business at hand.

Tillie took a sip and set down her cup carefully in its saucer before answering. She frowned. "It appears Seamus's death is being investigated as a murder."

Katie gasped and froze with her cup half way to her mouth.

"Did they tell ye this outright, Tillie?" Connor asked, his gut tightening.

"I may be an old biddy, but I'm not daft." Tillie pursed her lips. "The questions they were askin'. I know what they're getting' at."

"Oh, Aunt Tillie." Katie put a hand on her aunt's arm. "Who would want to…to hurt Uncle Seamus? He was the kindest man. He couldn't have any enemies. What motive would someone possibly have?"

"Aye, that he was." Tillie gave a soft smile. "But the *guarda* are lookin' for a correlation between his death and a few incidents of breakin' and enterin' here at the manor house a few months ago. 'Tisn't possible, so I told 'em. The only suspects bein' either an employee or a guest, and most guests move on after a few days. And I trust the staff. Besides, nothin' was taken. And…" She coughed into her napkin and took a moment to compose herself. "'Tis too dreadful to believe anyone wanted to harm my Seamus." She wiped her eyes.

"His death couldn't have been a murder, right?" Katie looked from Tillie to Connor. "Connor, isn't there something you can do? Can't you call someone?"

Connor had been deep in thought, watching Tillie and considering the next step to take in the investigation. The local authorities must have expended all their leads if they'd resorted to re-questioning the victim's widow. When Katie turned to him with her eyes so full of trust, he jolted. He wanted to do anything to maintain her faith in him. "Aye, and I'll certainly check into it, Katie."

She smiled, and the tension around her eyes relaxed.

Seeing her expression spread warmth through his chest.

"There you go, Aunt Tillie. Connor will—"

But Katie stopped speaking when Ian and Mrs.

Wilkie rounded the corner of the manor house.

The pair waved, making their way over.

Connor stood as they approached the table. He held Ian's gaze and, out of the corner of his eye, saw Katie tense.

"Hello, Kaitlyn and Tillie," Mrs. Wilkie said. "Is it teatime already? I just love teatime." She scooted into the chair next to Katie, beaming at Connor. "I don't think I've met you. Are you a friend of Kaitlyn's?"

Connor resisted the urge to glare at Ian, and he looked at Katie instead. "Aye, old and dear friends we are."

"Wow, Kaitlyn. How lucky are you? Am I right?" Mrs. Wilkie elbowed Katie, whose gaze was focused on the finger sandwich she picked at.

Tillie waved to Darcy who brought over a tray with another tea set. "And can I pour ye some tea, Mrs. Wilkie? Ian?"

"Nil. I thank ye," Ian said. "I'm just returning the lovely Mrs. Wilkie before I'm back to the courts." He pushed Katie's hair off her shoulder with the back of his hand, rubbing her neck.

Connor's jaw clenched.

"And we're off to the pictures tonight, aren't we, Kaitlyn?" Ian smirked at Connor.

Katie looked up. "Yep. I'll see you tonight."

Her smile looked a bit forced.

Ian let his fingers trail across her shoulder before he left.

Connor employed years of training to keep his face impassive.

Kaitlyn glanced at the table setting, and they were plunged into a moment of awkward silence.

Mrs. Wilkie leaned toward Kaitlyn. "I wanted to ask you about your necklace. Oh, you're not wearing it now… Anyway, I asked Ian where to find something like that, and he told me to ask you. The gold knot one. I just love how 'Irish-y' it looks, ya know? And yours is one of the nicest I've seen."

Connor's gaze snapped to Mrs. Wilkie. Her expression seemed innocently curious. The woman obviously didn't have the radar for social nuances. Was the question just a horrible coincidence? He looked back at Katie and saw the color drain out of her face.

She slid back her chair and stood, still not looking at any of them. "Excuse me," she mumbled. "I'm not feeling very well."

Connor reached a hand in her direction. "Katie, can I—?"

"Take care of Aunt Tillie." She rushed into the dining room.

"Poor darlin'." Tillie shook her head. "She's not been her happy self for the last few days. And this news must have been quite a shock."

Connor glanced at Tillie, and then toward the doors Katie had just gone through, debating over whether to follow. He had no doubt she'd not want to talk to him, and Tillie needed him right now, anyway. He sighed and sat again.

"You and Kaitlyn should join me and Ian for tennis sometime." Mrs. Wilkie spoke around a mouthful of finger sandwiches.

He had completely forgotten she still sat at the table.

Mrs. Wilkie winked and picked up another sandwich. "We're becoming quite the pair to beat."

Connor couldn't think of two people he'd rather spend time with less than Ian and Mrs. Wilkie. That was saying a lot, since he'd spent months at a time infiltrating drug rings and terrorist organizations, associating with the vilest human filth imaginable. He reached deep, miraculously found a smile, and forced his clenched muscles to relax. "That sounds grand."

Chapter 12

A few hours later, Connor waved to Fergus the groundskeeper as he walked around the perimeter of the pond, waiting for the inspector. He'd avoided this area of the property since his arrival but decided the time had come to shelve his emotions and focus on the case. The pond wasn't huge. Perhaps eighty meters across and deep enough for fishing and small rowboats kept tied up at the wooden dock. The water wasn't clear but rather murky. Reeds and grass grew along the bottom, and Seamus hired a special crew every year to clean out the vegetation to prevent the pond from becoming a bog.

He turned back to study the view of the manor house. In plenty of places the garden shrubbery obscured the path around the pond. That no one in the inn had seen anything that night, as he'd read in the reports, was no surprise. Looking toward the parking area, he waved at the approaching man and walked in his direction. "Chief-Inspector O'Scanlon?" he asked when he neared.

"Aye, and ye'll be Connor Flynn." The two men shook hands. "Here are the case files ye requested. Ye'll find background checks on guests and employees who were at the manor when the death occurred, and I'm at yer service, as I'm able."

"Thank ye." Connor took the files and appraised

the older man. He was small and ruddy looking with a stocky build, short crew-cut hair, intelligent eyes, and a bushy mustache. "And how long have ye been at the department in Tullybrae, then?"

"Short of a year." The inspector smoothed down his mustache. "I've come down from Galway to replace Chief MacMahon when he retired. 'Tis the first actual case since I've arrived that didn't involve a pub brawl or a missin' farm animal."

"Aye," Connor said, impressed by the man's competence. "And can ye tell me the specifics, then? Walk me through it?"

"'Twas near here that the body was found." The inspector led Connor around to a shallow, boggy bank on the other side of the pond. "Forensics couldn't isolate any footprints because of the amount of foot traffic on the property, but a sharp rock with blood was found near the dock. 'Tis still down at the lab if ye'd like to see it. The blood has been matched to the victim, but no fingerprints were found on the rock. The medical examiner confirmed the official cause of death was drowning. But the victim suffered a head injury, which we assume was the reason he didn't struggle or swim to shore."

Connor appreciated the inspector spoke of the case in clinical terms. His professionalism made it easier to distance himself from the fact they were discussing Seamus. "And show me where the rock was found, then."

The inspector nodded and led Connor to another area of the pond. "And 'tis here we believe Mr. O'Brien hit his head, whether 'twas an accident, causing him to become disoriented and fall into the water. Or more likely..."

"Someone knocked him out and threw him in." Connor finished for him. His body chilled.

"Aye, and 'tis my gut feeling someone did this. However, we've no evidence. No robbery was committed, and try as we might, we've been unable to determine a motive. The only reason this case is still bein' investigated at all is because of pressure from yer department, if ye'll excuse me sayin' so."

Connor nodded and scanned the area, reenacting the events in his mind. Once Mrs. Wilkie left them alone on the veranda, he'd spoken to Tillie at length, sifting out details the detectives had been unable to discover about that night.

From what she told him, he knew Seamus left the house around ten thirty. For him to take a walk late in the evenings wasn't uncommon. He'd been upset by a few phone calls earlier in the day, and although he hadn't discussed them with her, she thought they were the reason he couldn't sleep. Seamus's phone records had been thoroughly checked, but one number belonged to a disposable phone and was untraceable.

Connor imagined Seamus walking down the path from the house. Was he meeting someone? If he was, this place was perfect for a secret rendezvous. But if Seamus had been upset, would he be out here in the middle of the night? *Only if he thought the area was safe. Or only if he believed he protected Tillie.*

He visualized how the man he regarded as his uncle would have walked down the garden path then toward the docks. The area was open, with few places to hide. Connor retraced Seamus's footsteps in his mind. He would have paused at the edge of the garden with his back to the hedge, scanning the area, making sure nobody could sneak up behind him. Even if he felt safe, certain precautions were just second nature. Then he'd walk forward slowly, keeping his senses on high-alert, and if threatened, he'd have his weapon ready—Connor squinted at the inspector. "Was Seamus's gun holstered?"

"Nil. A weapon wasn't found on the body, though he wore a holster."

Connor's heart beat faster. "Sure, and Seamus wouldn't have approached a potential enemy without his weapon ready. Yer team searched the area, I take it."

"Scoured it dozens of times, searching for clues, we did." Connor and Inspector O'Scanlon both looked at the water. "And I've a feelin' ye'll need a diver."

Connor nodded and kept searching as the day elapsed. At nearly dark, he was almost ready to call off the search for Seamus's weapon.

The diver had been searching the murky pond bottom for hours. Darcy brought a basket of sandwiches for the group at suppertime.

Connor could tell the men were anxious to return to their families. Though he wanted to ignore it and focus on the investigation, he'd been distracted when Ian arrived in his old dilapidated hatchback to pick up Kaitlyn. The view of the Manor House doors was blocked, but Connor watched with a clenched jaw as they drove out through the gates a few minutes later.

He fought against the images that surfaced in his mind: Ian with his hand on Katie's shoulder, touching the back of her neck, smiling at her... Connor knew the date was none of his business, he shouldn't be obsessing about the two of them together, but not thinking about Katie enjoying time with another man was becoming harder. Ian had something that had once been his. Something precious, and Connor was desperate to win back Kaitlyn.

Things hadn't gone very smoothly between them, but if he asked, would Katie consent to spending time with him? Sure, they had history, but he'd remind her they were old friends. For the two of them to go to dinner wasn't entirely unreasonable.

What was his end game? Win her back just to prove to Ian that he could? Win her back then leave? He'd already decided against a long-term relationship—with anyone. So, why couldn't he stop himself from touching Katie? Flirting with her? Reminding her they'd had something once… He was being selfish himself.

An officer called to Connor, shaking him from his thoughts in time to see the diver had surfaced. Instead of clinging onto the boat to rest before diving again, he held up his hand to show a gleaming metal object and pulled off the mask revealing his expression of triumph. He brought the weapon to the Inspector who slid on his own gloves, took the gun by the barrel, and held it toward Connor.

When he saw the gun, Connor had the satisfaction of knowing his hunch had been correct. The weapon was definitely the right model. He nodded to the inspector.

"We'll get it identified and fingerprinted at the lab immediately." Inspector O'Scanlon peered at the gun then slid it into a plastic evidence bag that a detective held open.

A sinking feeling quickly overshadowed Connor's sense of success when he realized Seamus had his gun that night. Not only did he carry it, he had it unholstered. While that fact didn't prove whether or not he was murdered, it did prove he had been concerned for his life when he'd walked down to the pond.

Chapter 13

Late that evening, Kaitlyn and Ian walked from his blue hatch-back to the Manor House. She glanced toward the pond. Connor and the police had been down there earlier. What had they been doing?

Ian let go of her hand to swing open one of the heavy doors, and then stepping inside, left it partly closed behind him.

The night was uncharacteristically chilly for this time of year, and Kaitlyn held her coat tightly around her shoulders. She shivered and couldn't help thinking of the warm quilt on her bed. A housekeeper would have built a nice fire in the fireplace. Turning toward him, she smiled. "Thank you for a wonderful evening. I loved the movie."

"Aye, but I'll admit, concentrating on the pictures with such a fine bit o' stuff sitting next to me was difficult."

Kaitlyn pulled her coat tighter against the draft. She was usually flattered by Ian's compliments, but she found they didn't sit as well with her tonight. Their previously easy relationship was becoming forced, and Kaitlyn felt more uncomfortable around him.

He stepped closer and brushed her hair off her shoulder. He leaned forward to kiss her.

At the last minute, she turned her head so his kiss landed on her cheek. She took a step back. "I'd better get to bed. I'll see you tomorrow for my lesson, right?"

"*Níl.* 'Tis my day off tomorrow."

She looked down at her hands, feeling guilty about the disappointed look on his face.

"But I'll be checking in on ye. I'd be fierce sad not to see ye all day."

"Good night, Ian." Kaitlyn attempted a cheerful smile as he closed the door behind him. She knew she'd been rude. Being friends with Ian had been so much easier when he was content with them just being *friends*. As she walked across the great hall toward the stairway, she let out a sigh.

"Yer not attracted to him." Connor stepped out from the shadows next to the statue.

Kaitlyn jumped and spun when she heard the voice. "You startled me. What are you doing hiding down here?" *Has he been waiting for me?* She spluttered her words before regaining her composure. "And I'm *quite* attracted to Ian." *Well, pretty attracted anyway.*

"Yer body language tells a different story. Yer arms folded, leaning away from him. 'Tis something else ye were thinking about—anxious for him to leave."

She unfolded her arms and balled her fists at her sides, furious that he was so close to the truth. "I didn't realize you were an expert on body language."

Connor shrugged. "'Tis my job."

"Your job is to be a nosy busybody?"

His lips twitched. "I guess ye could say that. Reconnaissance sounds a bit more professional." He walked closer as he spoke. "Ye feel safe spending time with Ian Kerry, because ye feel nothing for him. Ye've been hurt before, and yer protecting yerself."

Kaitlyn raised one eyebrow and tipped her head.

"I'm afraid you're mistaken, and anyway, that's my affair, not yours. I do like Ian very much. He's thoughtful and kind. He doesn't hide in the shadows spying on people. And, he is very attractive." She spun on her heel and hurried up the stairs. Connor's footsteps sounded right behind her. Reaching the upper hall, she started walking toward her room. Connor's hand on her shoulder stopped her.

He turned her toward him. "Katie, will ye have dinner with me tomorrow?"

His tone seemed demanding instead of requesting, and the sound put her on the defensive. "I'm afraid I have plans." She looked toward the pictures on the wall.

"What plans?"

Part of her wanted to spend time with Connor, but the other part hung onto her pride, wielding it like a shield against being hurt again. "I don't think that's any of your business."

His gaze narrowed. "Break them."

She looked back, studying his expression. When he was a teenager, his gaze was intense, and that very look had made her feel like the center of his world. But today, it sent anger moving hot over her skin. "Excuse me?" She spoke slowly so he would have no doubt as to her meaning. "Connor, I don't want to have dinner with you."

He shrugged a shoulder, though his gaze was still fixed. "'Tis just for old times' sake. Ye wouldn't come all this way, and not have dinner with…" He leaned his head to the side, studying her face. His eyes squinted. "I don't think yer telling me the truth. Ye don't want to have dinner because ye still have feelings for me…and they frighten ye."

A jolt stiffened her posture. Although she shook inside, she somehow held his gaze steadily. "That was eight years ago, and you have a rather high opinion of yourself and your effect on women. I've hardly even thought about—"

Connor closed the space between them and slid his hands into her hair, lifting her face and pressing his lips on hers.

The act cut off her words and stole her breath. Heat radiated through Kaitlyn's body. Connor's lips were hot and the way they held hers set her heart racing. Her heart was light, as if this kiss was just what it had been waiting for. As if all the years of loneliness, of missing him, had vanished with a simple touch.

After just a moment, Connor pulled away.

His breath warmed her face. Kaitlyn sighed softly and moved forward, raising her lips to meet his once more.

But he had stepped back.

She opened her eyes and blinked as the fog that had clouded her mind was replaced by anger when she saw the look of triumph on Connor's face.

Hot tears filled her eyes, and she turned before he could see them. He'd just been proving a point, and she'd fallen for the gesture, leaving no doubt he was right.

He took her hand. "Ye do still care for me, Katie."

His eyes were unreadable as he studied her. Kaitlyn pulled her hand out of his grip. Her face burned, and her lips still tingled. She was humiliated by how easy breaking down the walls she had constructed so carefully around her heart was. "Connor Flynn, don't you *ever* do that again."

"Very well. I'll not kiss ye again unless ye ask me to." His voice was soft.

"I'll never…" She crossed her arms and clenched her fists, hoping he couldn't see them shaking. She needed to get away from him before completely melting down. "And I don't have feelings for you."

"If that's so, I'll be seein' ye for dinner tomorrow, then…"

"Fine." The single word was all she trusted herself to say. She could cancel tomorrow, but for now, she just needed to escape. Practically running the last few feet to her room, she let herself in and closed the door, sinking into her chair. The tears came now. What was Connor doing? What was this insane game he was playing? One day asking for his necklace back then the next day kissing her like *that* and inviting her to dinner?

She touched fingers to her lips that were still hot from his touch. Every single feeling she had tried to forget for all these years came pouring back with Connor's kiss. The kiss wasn't one of a shy teenager, but of an experienced man. She hurt at the thought of all the experience Connor had probably had. She wiped the tears off her cheeks. Was Connor only getting her to fall in love with him again, because he wanted to prove he could steal her away from Ian? She was being manipulated in a macho power trip. And she hated all she could think about was how right kissing him felt. *How pathetic am I?*

****

Connor let the shower water pound on his face. He was ashamed with himself for how he'd treated Katie. Kissing her in such a heavy-handed manner was inexcusable. He hadn't meant to do anything but ask her to dinner, but the thought of another man's hands on her made his blood boil. Standing next to her in the darkened hallway had robbed him of any reason. When she'd denied her feelings...feelings he could see plainly in her face...he'd acted rashly. In the past few years, rashly was all he knew, but in this situation that behavior was wrong. He was used to making swift decisions, following his instincts, and acting with force and purpose. In this case, he failed miserably. Katie wasn't one to be commanded, and he needed to step carefully, consider her feelings and not simply his own injured pride.

He closed his eyes, remembering the feel of her lips. The taste of her. Katie wasn't a skinny teenager any longer. Her wide eyes were no longer naïve. Her body was soft and curvy, her skin warm, and when she'd responded to his kiss, he'd nearly lost his head. He stepped out of the shower, toweling off, glad the cold water had done its job and calmed the hot blood that had pounded through his body.

Tomorrow, he'd make up his behavior to her. Dinner would be perfect. He'd take her to Lyon's Pub—where they'd gone on their last night together all those years ago. Surely, she'd remember how special their date had been. He needed a chance to explain, and she would realize everything he'd done had been to protect her. He'd see her smile again. He'd win back his Katie.

Chapter 14

The morning sun shone through Kaitlyn's window, and she groaned. She'd slept poorly, and that description was an understatement. Not only did she replay the kiss in her mind, she alternated between fear, dread, and heart-pounding anticipation when she thought about her dinner date that night. After giving up the battle and acknowledging sleep wasn't coming, she decided what she needed was fresh air and a chance to clear her head.

After dressing, she breezed through the kitchen for a thick slice of Irish batch bread then grabbed a bike from the garden shed and set off for an early morning ride. She'd been cooped up on the Manor House property—hardly leaving for over two weeks and was ready for some time to herself.

Breathing in the cool and slightly damp morning air, she pedaled past the guards at the security gates then continued into the small town of Tullybrae, smiling at the locals who were starting their day in the picturesque setting they most likely took for granted. She passed a farmer in a tweed hat and vest who was attaching an old work horse to his wooden plow, waved to women hanging their laundry on clotheslines, and stopped to wait as a shepherd led a flock of white sheep across the road.

She loved the town and outlying farms with their

stone houses and tidy yards. Many of the roofs were thatched with straw, and nearly all had smoke rising from their chimneys. Chickens pecked in the yards, neighbors chatted, and colorful flowers spilled out of gardens. Although the weather had turned cloudy and drizzly, a warm feeling of contentment settled over Kaitlyn with the slower pace of the Irish countryside. She could lose herself in the quaintness of this life and objectively analyze the mess of emotions Connor created.

After riding past the church on the edge of town, she paused at the crossroads to admire a shrine to the virgin. Set in the intersection, the statue was simple and white. In the states, she would be Mary or Maria, but in Ireland, she was called Máire. At Máire's feet and in her hands were plastic flowers and behind her stood a cracked wooden sign post with arrows pointing in different directions to give travelers their options. Kaitlyn could ride back through town to the manor house, follow the road down to the cliffs at Carrick Point, or take Four Mile Road up toward the old castle ruins. She chose the latter.

Kaitlyn started pedaling up the winding road, remembering the first time she and Connor came to the castle ruins together. She'd been giddy that he'd invited her. She'd just turned seventeen and had another year of high school, and he was nearly two years older, starting basic military training in a few months. Connor was confident and handsome and, for an unknown reason, he chose to spend the day with her.

She steered around a bend and caught a glimpse of the castle tower through the trees. The ruins sat on a high cliff with only a narrow ledge dividing the ancient castle walls from a terrifying drop-off. Most of the structure had crumbled to little more than loose stones marking the foundation among the long grass, but the tall tower still stood, with stairs that led around the outside of the curving wall. Over time, the ruin had seen different owners. Years ago, an enterprising farmer even refurbished it to use it as a stable for his animals.

As she rode, Kaitlyn tried to lose herself in the beauty of the scenery, the smell of a countryside washed clean by rain, and the wildflowers lining the road. She battled with her feelings for Connor. Everything about him was intense. But yesterday, when he played with the kids, she'd seen the carefree boy she'd known years earlier. As she caught another glimpse of the tower through the trees, eight years melted away, and she remembered everything as if it were yesterday.

Kaitlyn had leaned back, her elbows resting on the picnic blanket Connor spread in the clearing by the tower. He sat facing her, their legs nearly touching "You're telling me Finn McCool sucked his thumb?" she asked.

"Aye, his thumb, 'twas magic, containing all the knowledge in the world, and he sucked on it to learn anythin' a'tall." Connor winked and looked out toward the sea. His dark curls blew back from his face.

She studied his profile. He had a strong jaw. A man's jaw, she decided. She usually felt awkward and skinny around boys, but Connor made her feel beautiful and grown up. Even though he'd acted like taking her around Tullybrae had been his idea, she couldn't help but wonder if Aunt Tillie had talked him into it. Kaitlyn didn't want him to think she was staring, so she kept talking. "Finn didn't do it when anyone was watching, right? I mean wouldn't people make fun of him?"

Connor bent his knees, pulling them toward his chest and resting his arms on them.

When he looked at her with his blue eyes, his gaze nearly took her breath away.

"But Finn was a mighty warrior, Katie. Anybody who dared laugh at him would have been slain by his sword."

"I couldn't have helped myself. Just thinking of a huge warrior with a sword in one hand and his thumb in his mouth…" She giggled.

Connor grinned. He tipped his head. "Sure, and I don't think Finn would have slain ye, Katie. Not with yer lovely eyes and dimples flashin' at him."

Kaitlyn's face exploded in heat. She jerked upright, bending her head down to hide behind her hair and studied her fingernails, as if they were the most interesting thing she'd seen in a long time.

Connor reached forward, brushed the curls out of her face, and lifted her chin.

Her gaze was captured by his blue eyes, and her heart started racing.

He leaned closer and had gently pressed his lips to hers.

The clarity of her memory nearly stopped Kaitlyn in her tracks. Her first kiss—so innocent and sweet. Nothing like the kiss last night. *That* kiss was laced with desire and ownership and had aroused feelings she'd never felt before and frankly scared her.

Leaving the farmland behind, Kaitlyn rode up the steeper hill through the forest. The vegetation around her muted sounds eerily, but the dirt path was shaded and cool. As she rode closer, she made out a few cars parked in the long grass near the ruin. Tullybrae was so far off the beaten path that she was surprised tourists made the journey all the way to this remote spot. But what did she know? She was just a tourist herself.

As she was about to emerge into the clearing around the castle, a man stepped onto the road in front of her. Her heartbeat quickened, and nervous tingles attacked her insides when she saw his face and the way he watched her.

She judged him to be in his forties, rather stocky with closely shaved hair. He wore a black leather jacket. The way he stood—right in the center of the path—made him seem threatening. Kaitlyn braked and put her feet on the ground before she got too close.

"Out for a ride, are ye?" he asked with a smile.

Kaitlyn nodded. "Yeah. I was just headed up toward the castle." She stepped on the pedal and turned the handlebars a bit to the side, intending to ride around him.

He took a few steps closer, blocking her path. "These woods are dangerous. 'Tisn't safe to be here alone, especially for a lass as lovely as yerself."

His movement caused a flicker of panic. She stood, looking at him for a minute, unsure of how to respond. Was he threatening her?

"Well, off ye go, then." He made a motion as if to shoo her away.

Kaitlyn opened her mouth to argue, but the man's look hardened, sending a warning that spread tingles down through her fingers. Quickly, she turned around her bike and pedaled back through the forest and into the farmland. Her heart pounded. What had just happened? If the man wanted to rob her, or to attack her, he certainly had the chance, but his intention seemed more like he just wanted to get her out of there.

What was happening at the castle he hadn't wanted her to see? She'd heard stories about Druid ceremonies in the forest. Maybe that's what he was guarding. Whatever the reason, he'd made her feel uneasy. The feeling stayed with her, even after she passed Máire and the church, and rode again through the friendly town of Tullybrae with its brightly painted doors, beautiful flowers, and smiling people.

As she pedaled through the manor house gates, she saw a man on the road ahead pulling a cart piled high with branches. This time, she smiled. "Good morning, Fergus." She hopped off her bike and pushed it, walking next to him up the long, tree-lined driveway.

Fergus was a gray-haired man with a deeply lined face and a grandfatherly smile. His bright eyes twinkled when he saw her. "And if 'tisn't the lovely Kaitlyn. And where've ye been ridin' this fine mornin'?"

"I rode up on Four Mile Road, through the forest, and nearly to the castle."

His gaze darted toward her. "Darlin, 'tisn't safe in the forest for a young lady alone. Aye, the little people, they'll be leadin' ye away to their dens quick as a wink." Fergus glanced around.

He looked nervous as if he feared the faeries would hear him speaking about them. "I didn't meet any little people on my ride." Kaitlyn pressed her lips tight to force a serious expression. *Just one creepy guy, and nothing was magical about him.*

"Well, it's lucky ye were this time. But, it'll be

wise not to tempt fate again. Yer aunt would suffer a broken heart if somethin' was to happen to ye."

"And how would Katie be breakin' her dear aunt's heart, I'd like to know?"

They both turned when they heard Connor's voice.

He joined them from a side path.

Kaitlyn's stomach flipped at the memory of their last meeting. Her heart raced for the second time that day, but the reaction wasn't because she was afraid. In fact, she was actually relieved to see Connor. His steadiness eased her nerves.

"And if 'tisn't Connor Flynn lookin' ever more like a Jack-een." Fergus set down the handle of the cart to wrap Connor in a back-slapping hug. "How's she cuttin', boy-o?"

"Grand all together, Fergus."

Connor's face broke into a white-toothed grin that made Kaitlyn's heart flutter. He'd obviously been out for a run, and she fought against letting her gaze linger too long on his T-shirt that stretched across his broad chest or the shorts that showed off his muscular legs. "I'll say the grounds of Castle Hill have never looked finer." Connor picked the cart handle off the ground, causing his biceps to bulge, and walked with them back toward the garden shed. "Now, what were ye sayin', Fergus, about Katie temptin' fate?"

He waved his hand toward the road behind them. "Riding through the forest, she was. I warned her about the faeries and banshees. Lurk in the shadows, and 'tis a fool who ventures in there alone."

A muscle in Connor's jaw jumped. He looked back at Kaitlyn.

She saw his brows pinch together. *Was he mad? Or*

was every man in Ireland determined to treat her like a child?

"I know ye've heard about old Kellen Finnegan who lived just south of the river," Fergus continued. "Lured into a den of faeries, he was. Bewitched by their songs and dancing and food until, fifty years had passed him by before he knew it. Came wandering out of the forest with a beard as long as a saint's. And old Kellen not remembering a thing. Playing tricks is what they love, the wee folk, sure enough. Shenanigans and mischief." He turned toward Kaitlyn. "Ye'd best be watching yerself near that forest, lass."

"I'll be careful, Fergus," she said, smiling at the charming legend and the earnestness in his voice.

Fergus stopped at a hedge near the pond. "Well, and here we are. I've a bit more prunin' to do. I thank ye for pullin' my cart, Connor."

Connor set down the handle on the ground. "I'll be seeing ye at O'Malleys, I'll wager, Fergus."

"Aye, and I hope ye'll buy us a pint for old times' sake."

"That I will, Fergus. *Slán leat.*"

"*Slán agut.*" Fergus shook Connor's hand.

"Thanks for looking out for me, Fergus." Kaitlyn gave him a quick kiss on the cheek.

Leaving Fergus to his pruning, Kaitlyn and Connor parked the bicycle in the shed and started back toward the Manor House.

Kaitlyn felt Connor's gaze, and she cast around for something to say that would break the awkward silence. "What's a Jack-een?" She blurted.

"A Jack-een's what country-folk call Dubliners. 'Tisn't precisely a compliment." Connor shrugged one shoulder.

"Fergus has quite an imagination, doesn't he?" Kaitlyn shook her head and smiled, feeling a wave of affection for the older man as they walked through the front door and across the entry hall to the stairs.

"Katie, why didn't ye tell me ye were headin' into the forest? Dangerous, that place. Especially—"

"Especially for a girl alone." Kaitlyn ran her hand up the railing as they climbed the stairs. "I get it. I've heard the reprimand *twice* today, and it isn't even nine in the morning."

"'Tis true."

"I know." She sighed and looked out the windows of the hall as they passed. "The woods are full of scary little leprechauns who will take me away to their magical caves."

"Well, aside from the supernatural, ye'll find deep bogs, wild animals—" Connor stopped talking.

Kaitlyn turned from the window and glanced up at him.

Frowning, Connor stared at her bedroom door, which stood ajar. "Katie, did ye leave yer door open?"

"No," she said, reviewing her morning to be certain. "I'm pretty sure I locked it."

In a swift move, Connor shoved her behind him and moved to the doorway. He pushed the door open with the tips of his fingers.

Kaitlyn gasped at what she saw inside. Her bedroom looked like a tornado had hit. Drawers hung open, their contents strewn across the floor, sheets and pillows were crumpled in piles, furniture sat upended, and the mattress had been pulled off the bed and leaned haphazardly against one wall.

"Stay here, Katie." Connor moved to the bathroom, keeping his back to the door and peeking inside, then he opened the wardrobe. He finally nodded to signal that she could enter.

Holding herself tensed, Katie took a few steps into the room. Her heart sank as she surveyed the disaster in front of her. A knot tightened in her stomach at the violation of her space. Why would someone do this? *Who* would do this? Aside from her laptop, which was lying on the floor next to her bed, she had nothing of value. Tears pricked the back of her eyes.

"We'll be needin' to call up the *guarda*." Connor stood with arms folded, his gaze moving around the room.

"The police?" She shook her head, stepping toward him. "No way. Aunt Tillie has enough going on right now. I'm not making a big deal about this." She swallowed against the lump growing in her throat, hoping she wouldn't cry in front of Connor.

"I'm insistin', Katie."

He reached toward her, but instead of taking her hand, he put his arm around her shoulders, tucking her close against him as he dialed and spoke to the police. He ran his hand up and down her arm.

Kaitlyn leaned her head against his chest, not concentrating on his words as he spoke on the phone but on the comfort of being held and soothed. His body was warm, and the confident way he handled the situation pushed away her despair.

Connor kept his arm around her, and they walked down the stairs and out to the front porch. "The *guarda* are sendin' an inspector right away. They've asked that we not touch anything until they arrive."

Inspector O'Scanlon arrived half an hour later and took pictures of the mess.

Kaitlyn filled out a report and answered questions.

The other detectives looked around the room and dusted for fingerprints.

Once they left, Kaitlyn sank to her knees, exhausted, and tucked things back into her purse which had been upended in the middle of the floor.

"Yer sure nothin' was taken, then?" Connor squatted next to her, watching her put cash back into her wallet.

Her gaze traveled over the mess surrounding her. "Like I told the inspector about a hundred times, everything looks to be here. Just all over. I really don't have anything valuable—only my clothes and laptop. My purse and e-reader and passport..." She pointed to the various items around the room. "I didn't exactly pack a suitcase full of jewels and gold bars." She tilted her head and looked through partly-lowered eyelids. "I'm a schoolteacher, remember?"

Connor reached behind him and picked up a pair of lacy panties. "'Tis difficult to imagine any of my teachers wearing knickers like these." He gave a teasing smirk.

Kaitlyn grabbed them, heat rising in her face. "Connor, please leave."

Connor stood and walked around the room, stepping over clothes and around furniture while looking closely at everything. He paused when he saw a rose standing in a vase of water next to her bed. The flower seemed like the only thing that hadn't been knocked over or destroyed. "Is this from yer man, Ian, then?"

"Yes, it's from Ian. That's the kind of gesture a gentleman makes. He doesn't go pawing through people's underwear." She stuffed the underwear into her pocket as she walked over to a chair, righted it from where it had fallen, and slumped down, burying her face in her hands.

"And 'twould appear yer door wasn't forced." Connor spoke from the doorway. "The person who entered had a key. I'll talk to maintenance about replacin' yer lock."

She lifted her head. That Tillie had been away while the detectives were there was a relief, but soon enough, she'd return and learn what happened. "Poor Tillie. More stress is the last thing she needs right now."

"She's a strong one, Tillie is," said Connor. "Perhaps ye'll be wantin' to move to another room?"

"No." She glanced around at the mess. She didn't think moving to a different room would make her feel any better.

Connor picked up the other chair and sat. "Will ye be all right now, Katie?"

"I'll be all right."

"And did ye see anythin' suspicious today? Did ye talk to anyone besides Fergus this mornin'?"

"I did see this one guy…" she said slowly. "But he was too far away, he didn't have anything to do with …" Her voice faded as she waved a hand toward the room.

"And what *guy* would that be?" Connor's brow furrowed.

"I don't know. Just a guy up by the castle. He blocked the road and wouldn't let me get close." She shivered, remembering. "I don't know what he was protecting. But he creeped me out."

"And why did ye not tell me about this incident?"

Seriously? She lifted her head, raising her eyebrows. "I was a little distracted." She waved her hand around to indicate the room. "Plus, I didn't think it was any of your business, and I definitely didn't want Fergus to hear about it. The incident really wasn't that big of a deal."

Connor ran a hand through his hair. "This man, will ye tell me if ye see him again?"

"Yeah." She took a deep breath. "But I don't want to talk about it. I'll see you later, okay?"

"I'll stay and help set things to right."

She rubbed her temples. "Not necessary. Connor, I just want a nap, then I'll tackle this mess."

They both looked at the disheveled bed with the bedding strewn around the room. Connor lifted the mattress and adjusted it on the bed frame and then picked up a mess of sheets and started shaking to untangle them.

"Here." Kaitlyn took the bundle from him. "You don't have to do that."

"Katie, I know how to make a bed."

She started to pull apart the ball of sheets. And Connor grabbed a corner and helped untwist it. They spread the fitted sheet over the mattress, working efficiently together, tucking and folding the rest of the bed into place. Something about Connor's easy movements, and such a familiar task comforted her.

Connor set the last pillow on the bed a minute later, smoothed it and turned down the corner of the quilt.

The gesture was so simple, and yet it felt so

intimate. Heat flared in Kaitlyn's face again, and she busied herself straightening pictures on the walls. "I can get the rest of this clean-up taken care of. Thanks, Connor."

"Ye'll be all right, then?" He tilted his head to catch her eye. "I'll not be far away."

She nodded, feeling foolish for wanting him to stay.

"I'll come for ye at six then, shall I?" Connor began walking toward the door but stopped and picked up a dress from the floor. He turned toward her, cocking an eyebrow. "I wouldn't be disappointed to see ye wearin' this. I'd wager 'tis the perfect thing with yer lacy knickers."

Kaitlyn tossed a shoe at him, unable to stop the blush and the smile that spread across her face. "Good-bye, Connor."

"There's the first true smile I've won from ye in eight years, Katie," he said with a wink. "I'll be tryin' me fiercest to see it again."

Kaitlyn closed and locked the door behind him, leaning against it and allowing a tear to slide down her cheek. Knowing someone had been through her room was unsettling, and a little terrifying. That they hoped to find something valuable among her private things. Of course, nothing was taken. What was here to take? But knowing she hadn't been robbed did little to ease the nervousness she felt. Obviously, since they'd found nothing, she had to be nervous someone would return.

Pulling the bench from the end of her bed across the room and pushing it tightly against the door helped calm her a little. As did the image of Connor's smile and teasing grin. She needed to put him out of her mind. He'd been sweet today when she'd needed him. And that just made what she had to do more difficult.

Her breath caught. She was still in love with him, and she knew it. Worse, *he* knew it. But instead of letting herself be hurt again, she needed to take control. Tonight, she'd be firm and let him know in no uncertain terms she wasn't an insecure little girl whose heart he could toss around. She'd end the relationship for real and leave no room for him to misinterpret her resolve.

Chapter 15

Kaitlyn spent the remainder of the day in her room. Napping in the sunlight with the bench blocking the door gave a feeling of security. She was surprised at the way her heart sped when she considered leaving the safety of her locked room. When both Ian and Aunt Tillie called her, she used a headache as an excuse. She assured Aunt Tillie again and again she didn't need soup, just rest. Finally, the older lady left her alone when Kaitlyn told her she was having dinner with Connor that evening.

After taking a nap, re-folding her clothes, and straightening her room, Kaitlyn still had a few hours before her dinner date. She took her time, soaking in a hot bath, painting her nails, and straightening her hair. She put on a dress and a pair of rhinestone-studded strappy heels that made her legs look great but were far from comfortable. Luckily, she wouldn't be doing much walking tonight. She spent extra time with her eye make-up, achieving a dramatic smoky eye look, and leaned close to the mirror to carefully apply lipstick. Stepping back, she studied the entire effect. *Perfect.* She felt strong and beautiful and sexy. She'd need the confidence boost to hold her ground when she told Connor how she felt. Although she knew her motive was petty, she wanted to look amazing doing it.

At six o'clock sharp, she heard a knock on her

door, and her heart skipped. Not sure whether the reaction was because of whom she was expecting or knowing she still felt vulnerable after the break-in, Kaitlyn pulled away the bench from the door and opened it a crack. Seeing Connor's face did little to calm her nerves, and she opened the door wide.

"Ye look lovely, Katie." Connor looked her up and down.

She practically glowed under his admiring gaze.

His smile widened when he pulled a vase full of roses from where he'd concealed it behind the doorframe and stepped through the door. He strode across the room and set the grand arrangement in front of the small bud vase holding Ian's rose. "Much better."

When he turned, she tipped her head and gave him a flat look. "Really?"

"'Tis the kind of thing gentlemen do." Connor's lips quirked. "And I'll say it again, yer looking grand tonight, Katie." His gaze moved over her silky floral dress and stopped at her feet. "And yer shoes are…"

"Sparkly?" she offered.

"Aye, and they look like torture devices."

"You look nice, too," Katie said, too aware of his gaze, and her blush as she admired his all-black ensemble of a sport coat over a button-down shirt and slacks.

Connor smiled and offered his arm, "Shall we, then?"

She grabbed her purse and jacket and slipped her hand into the crook of his elbow. Connor's humor and charm had disarmed her. Try as she might, Kaitlyn couldn't quite hold onto the bit of anger she had been planning to use as a shield this evening.

The two started down the steps, and Kaitlyn was glad for Connor's arm. She needed all the support she could get on the steep staircase in her ridiculous shoes. And she wasn't complaining about feeling his bicep either.

Kaitlyn glanced up at Connor, expecting to see his profile, but her heart tripped when she connected with his gaze. She smiled shyly, lowering her lashes and looking toward the bottom of the steps. She nearly lost her footing when she saw Ian watching them.

Realizing how bad the scene looked, she pulled away her hand. She'd told Ian she was sick all day, and here she was, dressed to kill, and heading out for a night on the town with Connor. Had Connor seen Ian standing there? Is that why he'd been looking at her like that? He hadn't been enchanted with the idea of a night out with her. He was just happy for a chance to make Ian jealous.

Kaitlyn edged away from Connor as she walked down the last few steps. "Ian. Hi. I—"

Ian's gaze moved back and forth between Kaitlyn and Connor before settling on her. His usual smile had been replaced by narrowed eyes and pressed lips. "I was comin' to check on ye. Since ye've been ill today. But I can see I've no need to be worryin'."

"Yeah, I feel better now, and Connor's asked me to dinner." Her heart sank when she saw the hurt on Ian's face.

"Aye, we've important personal matters to discuss, Katie and I." Connor touched his hand to the small of her back.

"I'll not be keepin' ye, then." Ian started toward the front door. But he paused and turned back. "I shoulda told ye how fetchin' ye look this evenin', Kaitlyn. I assume yer not headed to O'Malley's pub dressed to the nines."

She scratched her arm and glanced at Connor. "Um, I'm not exactly sure where we're going."

Connor kept his even gaze trained on Ian. "I thank ye for checkin' on Katie, but we'd best be off."

"Good night, Ian," Kaitlyn said, as he stepped outside and disappeared into the darkness.

Connor held her jacket while she slid in her arms. Then he opened the Manor House door.

She glanced around, but Ian was nowhere in sight. Poor Ian. She hated that she'd hurt him. Her motive hadn't been intentional, but that justification didn't do much to drive away the tightness in her throat or the lump in her stomach. She'd have to apologize tomorrow at her tennis lesson and hope he'd be back to his happy self.

Kaitlyn walked around the car to the passenger side and opened the door before she saw the steering wheel and turned, blowing out a breath. "Oh, oops."

Connor stood behind her, holding up his keys. "Yer plannin' to drive, then?"

The sides of her mouth curled up when she saw his teasing expression. "I forgot." She followed him back to the *real* passenger door.

"I'd let ye drive if 'twould please ye." He opened the door.

"I wouldn't dare drive your car."

"And why not?" Connor leaned his arm across the open door.

"Well, because this car costs more than I'll make in the next three years." She slid into the seat.

Connor closed the door and walked around the car. He slid behind the wheel and started the engine before turning. "'Tis only a car, Katie."

"Maybe it's not a big deal to you, but it's the nicest car I've ever ridden in."

He shifted gears and started down the drive toward the Manor House gates. They waved at the security guards as they passed. "Are ye feelin' better now—"

Connor's phone rang. He checked the screen before turning to Kaitlyn. "Sorry, if ye'll excuse me for a minute, then. 'Tis my gaffer." He pressed the button and, with a wry smile, spoke into the phone. "Aye, Jack. Sure, and ye'd call the minute I step out with a lovely lady."

Kaitlyn could hear a man's voice through the phone but couldn't understand what he was saying.

"Yer certain, then?" Connor said.

Her nerves pricked when she heard his voice drop, all traces of his earlier humor gone.

He listened a little longer. "I thank ye for ringin' me with this information." He breathed out heavily, lines forming around the sides of his mouth. When Connor ended the call, he set his phone on the console and rubbed the back of his neck.

"Is everything okay?" Kaitlyn asked.

Connor nodded, his face still tight.

"So, what's a gaffer?"

He looked at Kaitlyn, and his face relaxed a bit. "'Tis my boss, he is. Jack. He's just called with new developments in a job I'm workin' on. Sorry I am to interrupt our evenin' with business."

Connor's smile wasn't the carefree expression from a few minutes earlier. "So, is your gaffer Jack a

Jack-een, too?" she asked.

"Aye, that he is, Katie." His face softened into a smile.

"Where are we going for dinner?"

"We've not many options in Tullybrae. With what happened today, I'd prefer to stay close to the Manor House and Tillie. And so Lyon's Pub 'tis, then. Ye remember, we..."

"We went there before," Kaitlyn said softly. An image of sitting at a scrubbed wooden table, while candlelight shone over his features came into her mind.

Connor nodded.

Kaitlyn turned to look out the window. She'd known tonight would be uncomfortable. Too much history existed between them to just pretend things were the way they used to be. She remembered Lyon's Pub. The establishment was a step up from the rowdy "local" where the citizens of Tullybrae gathered. Lyon's was where patrons went for more of an "evening out." Connor had taken her there on her last night in Ireland. Her gaze darted toward him, but he was focused on the road. Lyon's Pub was where he'd given her the pendant in the first place. Is this the reason he chose it?

Connor held open the door to the pub, and Kaitlyn stepped inside. Her mood was instantly lifted by the smell of warm food and the sound of music and laughter that surrounded her. She looked around at the crowd as Connor waved a greeting to the bartender. One face in particular stood out from the rest, and Kaitlyn's breath hitched when their gazes met.

She leaned toward Connor, momentarily surprised by how tall her shoes made her. He only had to tilt his head a little for her to whisper in his ear. "See that man there at the bar? The one with the leather jacket? He's the guy from the castle. The one who stopped me on the road."

Connor didn't look at the man, instead he took out his phone and told her to turn with her back to the bar and smile as he snapped pictures. He typed into his phone for a minute and then gave Kaitlyn a quick wink.

He'd gotten a few shots of leather jacket man, too. Kaitlyn was about to ask what he intended to do with the pictures but stopped when she saw Connor wave to someone.

A dark-haired server wearing an apron and maneuvering through the tables with a tray full of drinks smiled as she approached them.

"And if 'tisn't the long-lost Connor Flynn. We've not seen hide nor hair of ye for months. It's lovely to have ye back in Tullybrae." She turned her face for Connor to peck her cheek.

"'Tis grand to see ye, Brianna. And this is Kaitlyn Donovan."

"Aye, yer Tillie's niece from the states, then. And I'm so sorry about yer uncle, Seamus. He'll be missed, and that's a fact. But I'll wager the two of ye've come to honor him with a pint o' the black stuff."

"'Tis supper we're after tonight," Connor said, "Though I'd not say no to a pint. And, Katie, what'll ye be havin'?"

"Water." Kaitlyn did her best not to allow her gaze to wander toward where the leather jacket guy watched them from the bar.

"Yer in Ireland, Katie." Connor held her arm and turned her slightly so the man was no longer in her view. His gaze flicked toward the bar and then back. "To order water in a pub is a crime."

"I'll just have whatever you're having."

"Brianna, tell Tom to build us two pints, then."

"Find a table wherever ye like, and I'll bring yer Guinness." Brianna raised her tray above the heads of the other diners as she made her way toward the bar.

Katie watched her, and her gaze darted back to the man in the leather jacket, her stomach feeling prickly.

"Don't let him make ye nervous, Katie. Yer safe with me."

"I know. I just wish he'd stop staring." The pub was dimly lit, and the wooden floors were uneven. Kaitlyn wobbled slightly in her heels.

Connor held onto her elbow as he steered her toward a small table in the corner.

Once they were seated, and Brianna brought their drinks, Kaitlyn began to feel self-conscious with Connor watching her across the table. He looked so handsome and so self-assured as he scanned the room. She picked up a menu and started looking over it.

Connor took a swallow of his dark beer, and then leaned forward. "Katie, I've a need to explain myself. About the necklace. That's why I brought ye here tonight—to make things clear."

Heat crept up her cheeks. "You really don't have to make a big deal. I'd rather just enjoy the evening." She hated feeling so conflicted. Couldn't they just spend time together without dredging up old memories and realizing things didn't and wouldn't work out between them?

He glanced around the room. While people sat closely packed into the small room, the music and the voices surrounding them provided an opportunity for a private conversation to go unheard. "But I'll explain all the same." He took another drink. "The pendant was given to me by yer Uncle Seamus. 'Tis one of three. They're very old relics, and he trusted me with their keeping and asked me to never speak of them or show them to anyone. I don't know if even Tillie knows they exist." He leaned closer across the table. "I was young, and I was besotted with ye."

Kaitlyn's throat constricted, and she concentrated on breathing evenly. A flush heated her face. Though a myriad of emotions fought within her, the one that made its way to the top was anger. Anger at this entire situation pulsed through her body. That he was still hung up on the stupid necklace, and she still struggled with wanting nothing to do with him.

"Giving one to ye 'twas a mistake. Not because I didn't mean what I said to ye, but because possessing it puts ye in danger."

A twinge of fear pulled inside, but anger was still her dominant emotion. Kaitlyn pursed her lips.

He sat back, pushing out a breath through his nose. "And yer not believing me."

She set down the menu and gazed evenly across the table. "You're right. I don't believe you. That I still have feelings for you is obvious, and for whatever reason you're using them for some kind of ego-boost. I won't just go along with it and be all coquettish and mysterious. You wanted me to be upfront, and so I'll tell you the truth." She took a deep breath which did little to calm her racing heart. "Since I was seventeen, and I left for Seattle, I've thought about you every day. I've compared every man I met to you. I tried to move on and make a life with someone else, but I couldn't do it. I couldn't pretend with him when I still had hope for you."

She swallowed the lump building in her throat. "I've imagined various scenarios where we'd finally be together, and none of them involved you taking away my necklace in a cemetery. Or bringing me back here and telling me all the reasons why you should have never given it to me in the first place." She tapped a fingernail on the tabletop.

"I'm not an expert on men—obviously—but I do know they usually want what they can't have. I don't understand your motives, and I don't trust them. You stopped writing without any explanation, and I didn't hear a peep from you for years. When I finally do see you, the first thing you do is basically let me know whatever you'd felt for me is in the past. But then when you find out that I'm seeing Ian, suddenly it's kisses, flowers, and dinner, and now a crazy story to explain your behavior." She wiped at a tear that escaped over the rim of her eyelid.

Connor opened his mouth.

She put up a hand to stop him before he could say anything. To finally get her feelings out in the open was a relief. "Let me finish. I know I'm naïve about things like this, but I'm not stupid. I've been hurt too badly to put myself through this again. I realize you don't feel the same about me, and I'll save you the awkwardness of pretending you do." She took a deep breath and let it out slowly, lowering her shoulders.

"So, here's what I'm planning for the rest of the night. I'm going into the bathroom to pull myself together and fix my makeup. Then I'll eat an enormous plate of fish and chips, because I'm starving. Then we'll have a nice conversation about easy topics like the weather or movies. You'll drive me back to the Manor House, where you can walk me to the bottom of the stairs and shake my hand to wish me goodnight. When I'm gone, you can pat yourself on the back for your escape from such a needy, insecure person."

Kaitlyn stopped Brianna as she passed their table. "Excuse me, where are the restrooms...I mean, the toilets?"

Brianna took a second glance at Kaitlyn's smeared mascara, and she cocked an eyebrow, looking between the two of them. "Jacks are down that hall in the back."

"Thank you." She stood and walked through the tables without a glance backward. She lifted her head high, hoping she could hold on to her last shred of dignity until she made it to the restroom.

A man stood in the dark hallway. He watched Kaitlyn stop and look at the signs on the two doors.

One said *Fir* and the other said *Mná*. Great. She reached for one handle.

"It's *Mná* ye'll be wanting, miss." The man pointed to the other door. "Although I don't think the gents would be for turning ye away." He smiled.

She saw the dim hall light glint off a golden front tooth. "Thanks," she said, before walking into the restroom, closing the door and leaning against it. She let her tears flow freely now, but surprisingly, she was relieved. To tell Connor exactly how she felt was freeing. Where had that empowerment come from? Her shoes? This new attitude wasn't like her at all. She was more the "pretend everything is fine" type. Leaving smooth-talking, lady-charming Mr. Connor Flynn speechless…that was just the icing on the cake.

A sound that was a mix of a giggle and a sob escaped her throat. She felt light, as if a giant weight had been lifted. She walked to the sink and cleaned away the mascara she'd smeared all over her cheeks. The smoky-eye make-up was a superb mistake, but she fixed it the best she could and stepped back to look at herself in the mirror. Now, she was a new person. No more pining away for Connor, or daydreaming of him, or hoping…always hoping. He wasn't the guy she'd thought he was, and taking control of her heart was a relief. Closing this chapter was the first step.

She smoothed down her hair, squared her shoulders, opened the bathroom door, and stepped into the hall. But before she had a chance to react, strong arms seized her from behind, and a meaty, sweaty hand clamped over her mouth. Panic shot like needles through her body.

Chapter 16

Kaitlyn tried to scream, but the hand pressed tighter, and her teeth cut into her lips. Nobody would have heard her over the noise in the pub anyway. In the dimness of the hall, she struggled until another man approached, and she recognized his gold-toothed smile.

"I'll be askin' ye to come with us, miss." He spoke, opening his jacket to show a pistol tucked into his waistband. "We'd appreciate it if ye weren't to make a fuss." He lifted the weapon and examined it as he leaned closer.

Kaitlyn's knees weakened, and her legs shook.

"Now, can we count on ye to keep yer voice down, then?"

Blinking hard against her tears, she nodded. Kaitlyn should be looking for an escape or fighting back—how many times had she seen this exact scenario on procedural crime dramas?—but the sight of the gun froze her insides, and her mind went blank. When she was released, she swayed, and the man pulled her against him, keeping his arm around her as they walked through a back door and into the cool evening air.

He pushed her into the back seat of a car and slid in next to her, while Gold Tooth got into the driver's seat. Kaitlyn glanced at the face of the man beside her, and she stiffened when she recognized the man in the leather jacket. She scooted away and pulled on the door handle, but the door wouldn't open.

"Don't ye be leavin' just yet." The driver turned in his seat and smiled. "Ye've got something we're needin'." Leather jacket guy was watching her, seemingly content to let Gold Tooth do the talking. "Now if ye don't mind, I'll be askin' ye fer yer necklace."

Kaitlyn looked back and forth between the two men. Her sluggish brain had kicked back into gear, and her mind raced. So, Connor had been telling the truth about the necklace? A weight settled into her stomach. Connor had been protecting her all along. From this very thing, and she'd acted like a—she cut her thoughts short as the driver started the car and began driving.

Kaitlyn looked past him, figuring out which direction they were going. And how to escape. Why didn't she fight these guys? Everybody knew if an abductor took his victim to a second location, the chance of escape decreased. She should have left a clue for the police, dropped a shred of her hem or something they could use to track her. Or screamed. Why hadn't she made a scene? Or at least tried to attract attention? And Connor. How long before he knew she was gone? Would he think she had just left? Would he go back to the manor and not even wonder where she was? Would anyone come looking for her? Her breath came in quick gasps.

"Perhaps ye didn't hear me, Miss Donovan." Gold Tooth watched her in the rear-view mirror. "I asked for yer necklace."

Kaitlyn found her voice and spoke with a bravery she didn't feel, hoping to hide her terror. "I don't know what you're talking about. I'm not wearing any jewelry, and if you're robbing me, you're out of luck because my purse is back at the pub."

Gold Tooth stared at her in the mirror before letting out a theatrical sigh. "'Twas my hope that we'd not have to do this the hard way." His gaze shifted to his partner. "Retrieve the necklace, Lynch."

Terror spread through Kaitlyn's body, shooting pain in her fingers and toes as the man with the leather jacket—Lynch—scooted closer and reached for her. She pulled her knees to her chest and screamed for all she was worth, only to have her mouth covered again. His face was so close she could smell beer and grease on his breath. He pulled roughly on the collar of her dress, and she heard a tear as a shoulder seam ripped.

She kicked out, struggling in his grip as his hand felt around behind her neck and on the skin of her shoulder. His touch left her feeling violated and initiated another surge of panic. Pulling away, she sank lower into the seat, shielding her body with her arms and kicked out again. This time, she was rewarded with the sound of a grunt as her foot—or more likely a sharp heel—made contact.

Lynch pulled away.

Kaitlyn held her arms across her chest, trembling and fighting the sobs welling in her throat.

"She's not got it," he said. "What'll we do now?"

"She may not be wearin' it, but she knows where it is. I know of a man and an old lady who'll be willin' to trade it for her if she asks sweetly," answered Gold Tooth. "But for now, we'll follow orders and wait for the gaffer."

"Wait for how long, then?" Lynch grumbled.

"An hour. Four hours. I don't know. I'll not be one

to second guess the man. He'll come when he's ready, and not before. Our job is to bring Miss Donovan and her necklace safely to the meeting place and wait."

Kaitlyn watched out the window as they drove. The road was familiar. She'd ridden this way earlier this morning. She wasn't surprised to see they were headed toward the castle ruin. When Gold Tooth parked the car and turned off the ignition, Kaitlyn made up her mind to run. Her heart pounded and her muscles coiled, ready to make her move.

His partner stayed in the car next to her while Gold Tooth walked around to open her door. He pointed his weapon and motioned with it for her to climb out.

"We'll not be havin' any more trouble from ye, I hope." He shut the door behind her. He held onto her upper arm and led her toward the tower ruin. "I'd not like for a pretty lass such as yerself to be makin' the same mistake as yer uncle, then."

Kaitlyn froze.

Gold Tooth tugged on her arm to get her walking again.

Cold ribbons of dread spread from her chest. Her fingers tingled, and her knees went soft again. Had these men killed Seamus? Did they think he had the necklace? Had Seamus died to protect the relics Connor had talked about? To protect Connor perhaps? The need to escape, to warn Connor, were her only thoughts. She looked around frantically. Not that she knew what she was looking for. What she needed was a plan.

Gold Tooth led her up the tower steps.

Kaitlyn jerked away her arm.

He grabbed onto her again. "Come on, girly. I thought we'd agreed ye'd behave yerself."

Kaitlyn peered up at the steep stone steps that wound around the outside of the tower, fighting to keep her panic at bay. "Please don't make me go up there," she whispered.

"It's safe in the tower, to be sure. And a lovely view of the sea ye'll have while ye wait for..." He looked at Kaitlyn, squinting and tipping his head. "And what is it that has ye frightened, then? Ghosts? Banshees?"

Kaitlyn didn't answer. She was afraid if she opened her mouth she'd be sick. When he pulled her up the staircase, she closed her eyes to avoid looking over the cliff's edge and held out her hand to feel the curving wall of the tower. She leaned as close to it as she could. Her shins and toes scraped and banged against the uneven steps as Gold Tooth practically dragged her up the stairs and into the room at the top.

He pushed open the old door, which had probably been installed by the same farmer who'd used the ruins for a barn. Kaitlyn moved as far away from the collapsed roof and missing wall as she could, doing her best to breathe calmly when she thought about how high they were. *It's only my imagination. The tower isn't really swaying.* She sank to the floor, trying to lower her center of gravity, and closed her eyes in an attempt to dispel the feelings of dizziness and vertigo that plagued her in high places.

"Go on and make yerself at home. Just so ye know, the door doesna lock, though I don't think I'll need to be worryin' about ye tryin' anything."

She heard the door close behind him and hugged her legs to her chest. Tears rolled down her cheeks, but she didn't care enough to brush them away. She lifted her head to glance around at the small space. Then quickly put it back down between her knees to keep herself from hyper-ventilating. She was cold, scared, and more than anything, disappointed in herself. Instead of planning an escape, leaving clues, or using self-defense, she'd panicked, cried, and nearly fainted. Now she sat, huddled in a ball in an unlocked room, too terrified to move.

Chapter 17

Connor took another sip of his Guinness and set the mug back onto the water ring on the table. He moved the glass around, making the ring grow wider. He looked around the pub. The man Kaitlyn had been worried about had left through the front door ten minutes or so ago, and Connor had moved to the window to record his registration plate number and make sure he had indeed driven away. Aside from locals, the only other people he recognized were Mrs. Wilkie, and an older man Connor assumed was her husband, sitting at a table close to the front door. He wondered whether he should check on Katie. She'd been gone nearly twenty minutes.

Tapping his fingers on the table, Connor waited for Jack to reply back to his text, hopefully with positive identification and information on the man at the bar. He continued to try to come to grips with Jack's phone call. They'd learned the weapon they'd found had been confirmed as belonging to Seamus, and additional fingerprints were still being identified.

He pushed his chair from the table, leaning back and resting his ankle on his other knee. Kaitlyn's words replayed in his mind. The things she'd said had pierced him. They'd come so close to mirroring his own feelings, and he'd wanted to hold her and tell her they'd figure it out, that the two of them could be together, but he knew it wasn't true. She would return to Seattle in a few weeks, and he'd go back to Dublin and then on to a new assignment somewhere.

Too much time had passed, and he only wished he'd handled the situation better years ago. Even a stupid teenager should have known no future was possible for a long distance relationship after a summer romance. Now, too much history existed between them to forget, and even harder to forgive. Wishing for a future together was hopeless. Their lives had moved in different directions. They wanted different things. Katie wanted a family, and he wanted…well, he *had* a career. A great one that he'd worked hard for. And what kind of husband and father would he be if he was gone for months at a time? A relationship—a marriage—just wouldn't work. He could never give her what she wanted. And Katie deserved more…

Somehow, Seamus had done it all. He was a top agent, a loving husband, and a father to Connor. He was missed when he was gone, but he'd made the time when he was home special. Connor wasn't Seamus.

But being with Katie again changed everything. He wasn't prepared for the power of his feelings. Without him realizing, she'd always been in the back of his mind, and now here she was, and the feelings he'd just explained away as bittersweet nostalgia from their first romance were deepening into something that scared him. Could he move on this time? Thinking of life without her left an emptiness inside that bordered on painfulness.

Brianna delivered their food. "And is there anythin' else I can be getting' for ye, then?"

The smell of supper made his stomach growl.

"Aye, if ye'd not mind. Kaitlyn…she's in the lavatory and has been for a fair while."

"Had a bit of a spat, did ye?" Brianna smirked. "Sure, and I'll pop in and make sure she's all right, then."

A minute later, Connor watched as Brianna wove through the tables toward him. Her pitying look made his throat thicken. The idea of Katie crying in the toilet sunk a heavy weight into his stomach. He rubbed the back of his neck with his palm. "She's still upset, then?"

Brianna shook her head. "Connor, I'm sorry. She's gone."

Connor bolted from the chair and rushed down the back hall of the pub, shoving open both lavatory doors as he passed, not caring who he offended. He ran out through the back exit, cursing when he still saw no sign of her. Why had he let her out of his sight? How could he have messed up things this badly? Her bedroom was broken into earlier today, a suspicious man who threatened her disappeared the same time she did, he learned new evidence of Seamus's murder, and he'd still let her leave alone. Connor cursed and smashed his palm against the stone on the side of the building. The pain in his hand helped clear his mind. He needed to calm down and consider his options.

Brianna stepped out of the door behind him, handing him Katie's coat and purse. "I've known ye to break many hearts, Connor Flynn, but 'tis the first I've seen ye so upset about it."

"Did ye see her leave?" He scanned the area.

She shook her head and motioned for him to follow. "Come, we'll ask, then."

He followed Brianna around the corner of the pub and saw a small group of employees taking a smoke break.

"Howzit?" She waved to the group. "Connor's lookin' for a lady. May have left through the back here."

Connor stepped closer. "She'd be wearin' a blue floral dress—"

"And fierce silver shoes." One of the women interrupted him.

"A bit scuttered she looked." A teenage boy spoke up. "Probably had too much o' the good stuff, and her man, he was helpin' her to the car—a black sedan. Over there."

Connor's gut hardened as he glanced toward where the boy pointed.

"His mate drove, I think," the woman added.

"Two men were here, then." Seeing their nods, Connor continued, "Did ye notice which direction they drove?"

The teenager pointed away from the manor. Toward the church. And the woman nodded.

"I thank ye for yer help." Needles of panic pricked in his chest as he dashed to his car.

With two abductors, Katie's chances of escape dropped significantly. He threw her purse and jacket into the passenger seat and turned onto the main road, following his instinct. They'd have no reason to take Katie back to the Manor House. Katie had seen the man in the leather jacket on Four Mile road, near the castle, earlier this morning. Connor decided that was the best place to start his search.

His phone rang, and he glanced at it. Jack. He

didn't have time for Jack right now. Parking his car on the side of the main road about a mile from the ruins, he did his best to conceal it behind a rock wall. He grabbed Katie's jacket and hiked on the smaller access road through the forest until he could see the ruins and the black car parked in the wide clearing near the tower. Connor crept closer and took cover behind a thicket, where he could observe and assess and come up with a plan. He studied the men.

They sat on the ground, casually leaning against the car and playing cards.

No sign of Katie. Connor figured she was most likely in the top room of the tower—the only structure with a door. He imagined the room with its collapsed roof and crumbling wall exposed to the sheer cliffs below. With her intense fear of heights, Katie had to be terrified. He surveyed the area a moment longer and decided his best chance at remaining unseen would be to wait until nightfall, which gave him a little over two hours.

Settling back against a soft swell of earth, Connor pulled out his phone. He dialed his voicemail and listened to Jack's message:

Connor, I don't know what is going on out there, but ye'd best mind yerself. The results on the prints from Seamus's gun were identified as belongin' to Robbie Lynch. He's a member of the Provos and one of the most-wanted men in Ireland. Not to mention he's the proud owner of a criminal record the likes of which I've not seen in all my years at the agency. Lynch is believed to be responsible for assassinations and bombings in Northern Ireland and Britain.

Can ye imagine my surprise when I saw ye'd sent

me a picture from a lovely pub, and one and the same man 'twas? Lynch...he's a hired thug, not a mastermind, and ye'll be needin' to discover who he's workin' for if ye'll be findin' the motive behind Seamus's murder. I'll not need to tell ye to watch yerself. I know yer doing good work, and sendin' in a group o' agents would most likely blow yer cover. I'm trustin yer judgment. I'll not interfere until ye ask for help. But please be careful, keep me informed, and watch yerself around Lynch. And whoever he's workin' with.

Connor ended the call and tapped his phone against his leg. Now he knew who'd killed Seamus. His stomach clenched, and his breath came heavily. He reached under his coat and fingered the pistol holstered below his arm. His first instinct was to take out both men in a surprise attack. But killing them would only satisfy his need for revenge. He'd not discover the men's plan nor who they worked for. Kaitlyn and Tillie would still be in danger. He needed to figure out who knew about the relics, who was behind this, and how to stop them from finding the treasure. *When did my life start soundin' like a scene from a pirate book?*

Half an hour remained before dark when two additional cars arrived, parking beside the other. Four more men got out.

Connor wished he was close enough to hear what they said over the sound of the surf hitting the cliffs. They all settled in, joining Lynch and his friend in their game of cards. If Connor's priority hadn't been rescuing Katie, he'd give nearly anything to know what or whom they were waiting for.

Chapter 18

Connor crept across the darkened clearing, tucking Kaitlyn's jacket into his waistband. Once he reached her, she'd be cold in the thin dress. About fifty yards of flat land stretched between the forest and the tower. He stayed in the shadows from the trees as long as he could, knowing he only had a small window of time before the moon appeared. When he had no choice but to cross the open field, he stayed close to the ground and moved slowly—not taking any chances of being spotted.

The men had turned on their cars' headlights to illuminate their card game.

Connor did his best to use the direction of the light to keep himself practically invisible. Finally arriving at the far side of the structure, he made his way along the ledge between the tower wall and the sheer cliff, turning his feet sideways to balance on the narrow shelf. When he estimated he was beneath the hole in the tower room, he started climbing.

The mortar between the stones in the wall was weathered away, and Connor counted on using the spaces to climb the thirty-foot wall. Hearing the waves crashing beneath him at the base of the steep cliffs, he gritted his teeth. Losing focus wasn't an option. He needed to get to Katie. He was her only hope.

Pushing the toe of his shoe into a gap, he slid his

hand over the rough stone, shifting his weight onto one foot while he lifted the other and then used his arms to pull himself up. Clouds covered the moon, and he felt for the gaps that would hold his weight. He reached with his right hand, pressing it into a cavity and shifted his weight, only to have a chunk of the rock crumble beneath his fingers. Frantically, he grasped for another handhold and finding it, hung motionless for a moment until his heart stopped racing. The sea wind pressed him against the wall. When he'd calmed himself, he started again, feeling across the coarse rocks, finding gaps, and hauled himself up. Finally, he reached the hole in the wall and climbed over the edge into the tower room. "Katie?" he whispered as he looked around the dark space.

"Connor?" Her voice shook. "I'm here."

By the moonlight, he spotted Katie sitting against the far wall, hugging her legs to her chest. Kneeling next to her, he drew her into his arms and felt her trembling. He wrapped her jacket around her as she leaned her head on his shoulder. "I've got ye now. Yer safe, Katie." His gaze moved over her tear-streaked face and down to her torn dress. "Did they hurt ye?"

She shook her head, nestling her body closer.

He heard her teeth chattering.

"How did you find me? I was so scared that no one would—"

"We've no time to talk. Come, ye'll have to climb down the wall."

"Are you kidding me?" Her voice rose.

"Ye can do it, Katie girl. I'll help ye."

"Connor, I can't even stand or look over in that direction. You know how I am with heights. Can't you call Irish 9-1-1? Or we could hide or…"

He lifted her chin to see her face. She shook against his hand. The fear in her eyes firmed his resolve. He'd do anything to keep her safe. "Listen. Katie, I can protect ye, but six men are outside, and I can't guarantee we'd make it if they see us. Our only chance is to climb down the wall. Do ye understand?"

She shook her head. "They just want the necklace. Can't you give it to them? Then they'll let us go."

He moved his other hand to her face, his thumbs wiping away the tears that covered her cheeks. She cried but wasn't hysterical, and her condition gave him hope that she'd listen to reason. "Do ye really think they'll let ye go? Did ye see their faces? Overhear any of their plans? Ye can identify them to the authorities." He leaned forward, looking intently into her eyes, and pressed his forehead on hers. "This path is our only chance. I'll not let ye get hurt. Can ye trust me then, Katie? I just found ye, and I'll not lose ye again."

He watched her eyes and saw a flicker of determination. "There's my brave girl. Ye'll need to focus on me, Katie. And not think on anythin' else. I'll keep ye safe. Do ye understand?"

Katie closed her eyes and nodded. "I'll try."

"Ye'll try, and ye'll do it because ye can, Katie. I'm askin' ye to put yer trust in me, but I'm tellin' ye I'm trustin' in ye, too. Are ye ready?"

She opened her eyes and took a deep breath then nodded.

For a moment, Connor held her gaze. The Academy taught various mental strategies for overcoming fear, and he'd used them all at one time or another. "When a thought comes into yer mind that gives ye any fear, ye must immediately replace it with a positive one. Ye'll need to make a conscious effort, Katie. Focus on yer thought replacement. Have ye a positive thought?"

Katie pulled her brows together.

He glanced toward the door, listening for sounds of the enemy's approach, but he kept calm for Katie's sake. "Tell me."

"I'm thinking of something my mom used to say. I can still hear her voice in my head. If I was afraid of something, she'd tell me, 'Keep your chin up; hold your head high. You'll never know what you can do until you're brave enough to try.' "

If Katie's ma had been there, he'd have kissed her. "'Tis perfect, that. Ye must concentrate on yer ma's voice tellin ye to be brave when fear enters yer mind. Here's where it's important ye trust me. There needs to be no question in yer mind when I tell ye somethin'. Concentrate on my voice, believe what I tell ye, and focus on it. Can ye do all that, Katie?" He pulled her up, holding onto her shaking hands, and led her toward the hole in the wall.

Katie straightened her shoulders.

He saw her lips pull tightly in a determined expression as she held his hands and followed. Connor helped new recruits in similar situations, but the stakes had never felt so high. His chest was tight, but he gave Katie a confident smile and pressed a kiss on both her hands. "Now, I need ye to imagine a wall with a ledge that's only about a foot or so off the ground. 'Tis an old one, this wall, with gaps between the stones, but 'tis strong. Now, turn around, Katie, and hold onto the wall. We'll be playin' a game, scootin' along it, our feet never more than a foot above the ground. Did ye ever play this game as a girl?"

Katie stared straight ahead, her breath came quickly, and her lips were tight.

He held onto her arms and eased her over the edge of the hole, making sure her toes were securely balanced on the lip of a stone. Then he quickly climbed out next to her, lowering himself so his feet were below hers and his face was close enough so she'd hear him over the sound of the crashing waves below. He glanced down once and said a silent prayer. *Please, God. Ye've given me another chance with Katie. 'Tis my fault she's in danger. Help me use my trainin' to save her.* "Good, Katie. Now slide yer left foot to the side. Just a bit. Ye can almost feel the solid ground just beneath ye. Next, slide yer other foot. Now, let's scoot yer hands a bit lower."

With stiff movements, Katie followed his instructions.

He winced every time she pressed her bare-toed shoes into another space. The wind from beneath blew her hair around her head, and her skirt flapped all over the place.

Concentrating so hard had to be mentally straining. Eventually, she'd lose focus, and he wanted to get her as far around the wall as he could. Only a little farther to her left, and a fall would mean dropping thirty feet and possibly breaking her leg instead of tumbling down the steep cliff.

"Yer doing perfectly, Katie. Slide yer foot a bit down and to the left." That he couldn't see around her frustrated him. *Did she have a good shelf to rest her weight on?* He didn't have a strong enough grip to catch her if she fell. "Now the other. And can ye still feel the solid ground so near, 'tis only a step beneath ye. Move yer hands to the left. Aye, and down a bit more." The tension in his chest loosened the farther they moved around the tower, but he still worried about the drop to the ground.

In the moonlight, he saw beads of sweat rolling on her face and knew, physically and mentally, she had to be nearing exhaustion. "Katie, now we'll climb downward. 'Tis a short wall, so close to the ground. Close enough ye can nearly feel the grass behind ye. Down a bit more, Katie. Yer hands first, one at a time, and then yer left foot."

Connor spoke calmly, knowing his voice was the only thing keeping Katie from panicking and dropping off the wall. He watched as she balanced on her toes. Those bloody shoes were sliding so much he wondered if he should have just had her take them off. The rough rock would have most likely cut her feet, and he'd chosen the lesser of two evils but second-guessed his decision.

The pads of his fingers burned as he waited for her to find another good grip. Then he moved down his hands so he stayed close enough she'd hear his steady stream of encouragement over the roar of the waves. Katie's arms shook, but her feet were still at least ten feet off the ground. "Just a bit more, Katie girl." He saw her blink rapidly and knew she was almost at the end of what she could do. Hearing a noise above them, Connor glanced upward, directly into the face of Robbie Lynch looking down through the gap.

Lynch's gaze swept the rocks below, before he turned his head and saw Connor and Katie. Lynch's eyes narrowed into a scowl as he reached into his coat and pulled out a gun.

Connor grabbed Katie around the waist, pushed off the wall, and they hit the ground, rolling. The only thing louder than Katie's screams was the sound of a gunshot that split the air. The impact of their fall was softened by the grassy soil beneath the tower. Katie's frantic screams would alert the entire group to their location. Connor jerked her to her feet, pressing her against the tower wall with a hand over her mouth. Before he drew his weapon, he looked her over quickly to make sure she wasn't hurt.

Shielding her with his body, he turned, took aim, and shot back at Lynch, who'd had to lean a ways out of the window to fire at the awkward angle. A grunt and a curse sounded over the noise of the surf, making Connor assume his bullet hadn't missed. "Katie, we have to run." He bent down and pushed the ankle straps of her shoes over her heels then gave up with a curse, grabbing the long heel in his hand and cracking it off and repeating with the other.

Her face looked ashen, her breathing rapid, and her gaze darted around like a frightened animal. Connor shook her shoulder.

Blinking, she focused her attention on him.

He tugged on her arm. "Now, Katie. Run." The sound of another gunshot and men's voices jolted her into action. The two tore across the field, and he pulled her forward into the forest.

In her broken shoes, Katie stumbled a few times and once cried out as she tripped and slid over rocks and branches.

Connor heard the confused shouts of the men

behind them become muffled by the trees. They were still close. He scanned the area for a place to hide. A few minutes later, he stopped next to a moss-covered log. "We'll hide here."

"No." Katie panted.

In the moonlight, he saw her reach down to unbuckle her shoe that hung askew by the thin ankle strap. The other must have broken off as they ran.

"We have to keep running. They have guns. They'll shoot us. We need—"

Her voice was high-pitched and panicked. He kept his calm. "Katie, we'll not outrun them. Not without yer shoes. Hiding is our only chance."

Katie's breathing sped up, and she wrapped her arms around herself. "I think they killed Seamus."

In spite of the immediate danger, he paused and put an arm around her shoulders, knowing how upsetting the realization must be. "I know, Katie." Connor took her hand and pulled her down to the jagged opening. "We'll have to crawl inside."

She drew back. "What about animals? Snakes?"

"No snakes." He turned on his phone and shone the light into the hollow log then gathered handfuls of bushy branches and the broken shoe. "'Tis safe, Katie. Hurry." Grabbing her around the waist, he pulled her against him and eased the two of them feet first into the tight space. The inside of the log wasn't smooth, and sharp edges of the wood snagged and pulled at his clothes. He couldn't imagine how badly scraped Katie's bare legs were getting, but she didn't complain. Thank goodness, she had her jacket to protect her back and arms. She shook and her skin felt cold, and he worried she was going into shock.

Once they were completely inside the rotted-out log, he reached up and pulled in the clump of branches above their heads, blocking out the rest of the light and hopefully concealing their hiding place. The smell of decaying wood clenched his gag-reflex. Connor kept one arm around Katie—not that he could have moved it if he'd wanted to in the cramped space. The other held his weapon directed toward his feet.

Katie trembled. She laid her head on his shoulder, her body pressed against his. Both of her hands held fistfuls of his jacket. "Connor, why do you have a gun? And what—"

He heard noises outside. "Whist."

"Whist? What is a Whist?"

Katie's voice sounded high, and he could hear the fear it held. He tightened his arm around her. "Whist means 'quiet'. *Listen*," he whispered.

She turned her face, pressing it into his shoulder.

Connor held her close, his hand cupping the back of her head. In the little space he had, he shifted his shoulders to bend his other arm, holding his gun by his cheek and aiming it toward the opening above their heads.

"They'll not have gone far. Not unless they reached the access road."

"I told the gaffer we should just take care of these two, and the old lady would give us what we need right away. If we put the screws to her, she'd not last as long as her husband."

"Aye, but she may not know what we're lookin' for. Then where would we be?"

"I'll head to the access road with O'Connell. Lynch is injured, so ye take the other lads and search the forest—make yer way to the main road. We need to find them before they call out the *guarda.*"

The voices grew softer, and Connor lowered his weapon, sliding on the safety but setting it right next to him in case he needed it quickly. "Are ye alright now, Katie?" He brushed his fingers along her cheek and pressed a kiss against her hair in the dark.

Katie trembled. Her body was rigid. She turned her face.

Her warm breath tickled his neck.

"I'm just so scared. What if they come back? Will they hurt Aunt Tillie?"

"Don't worry yerself anymore. I'll take care of ye. We'll figure out how to keep Tillie safe, too." Connor shifted to free his arm and rubbed her shoulder through her jacket.

"Why do you have a gun?" Her voice slowed.

Her adrenaline rush was wearing off. "We've a lot to talk about, Katie. But 'twill keep. 'Tis rest ye need, now."

Kaitlyn scooted down and nestled her cheek into the hollow beneath his shoulder. Her body softened as she relaxed, and her breathing steadied. "Connor?" She yawned.

"Aye, Katie?"

"You ruined my favorite shoes."

He chuckled softly. He'd take her jokes over her fear any day.

"I'm sorry I didn't believe you about the necklace."

"I'll not hold it against ye for bein' skeptical."

For a few moments, they were both silent. He thought she might have fallen asleep.

"Can you believe I did that?" she asked. "I climbed

down from the tower?"

Her voice was softer and sleepy. He smiled at the pride in it. "I never doubted ye'd do it."

"I couldn't have done it without you."

His fingers trailed down her cheek, brushed around her neck, and threaded through her hair.

She shifted against him, her waist pressing against his hip, and a leg moving over his.

Heat spread through his blood.

In the tight space, she stretched out her arm, resting it over his chest.

His muscles jumped as her fingers moved along his side.

Her body melted into his. Again, she yawned. "Connor?"

"Mmm?"

"Thanks for coming for me."

His throat felt thick as he realized just how close he'd come to losing her. He squeezed her tighter. "I'll always come for ye, Katie."

****

Connor lay in the dark log, his arms around Katie, listening to the sound of her breathing and feeling the soft warmth of her body pressing against his. She seemed so fragile, and yet, he'd seen a strength today that amazed him.

Engines sounded, and he figured the group looking for them assumed they'd escaped and rushed to leave before the authorities arrived. The escape had been a close shave, and he and Katie were in no way safe. He thought through his options and came to the conclusion he needed to call Jack. The only way he could guarantee Katie and Tillie's safety would be to make a deal. He'd need an "in" with the terrorists. Making these kinds of connections was what he did. He knew how to infiltrate their groups. All he needed was a phone number. This way, the only person in danger would be him. The problem was, he'd have to keep the plan from Katie. She couldn't know he was working with their enemies. Not if he hoped to maintain the integrity of the investigation. But, she'd never agree. The scheme was too risky.

Sighing, she shifted in her sleep.

Warmth welled up inside him. He'd realized when he saw Katie in that tower, she was what mattered most in the world. He'd risk everything to protect her. The way the situation looked now, risking everything was exactly what he'd have to do.

Chapter 19

Kaitlyn's mind was murky. The pain in her feet and legs awakened her, but she struggled to remember why she was so tired. Why was the space so dark? She jolted as the events of the night before paraded through her mind like scenes from a James Bond movie. Only this one had a pretty pathetic leading lady. When she remembered where she was, her heart did a slow roll. She lay sandwiched between the rough wood of the log and Connor's solid body, feeling the heat of his arms through her jacket and inhaling his delicious smell—tainted only slightly by the odor of mold that permeated the log.

She slowly bent her arm, opened her hand, flattened it, and pressed it against his chest. Her other arm lay smashed beneath her. She sighed. She'd dreamed so many times of waking up exactly like this, in Connor's arms. Obviously, this scenario wasn't what she'd had in mind. She pushed away her foolish thought. Try as she might to savor the moment, she knew in reality, this embrace wasn't a lover's. His hold was more like a soldier protecting a child. An action made necessary by proximity and an extreme situation, and she deluded herself to pretend the gesture was more.

The burning in her legs and the throbbing ache in her feet chased away her little romantic daydream. She moved her top leg and sucked in a breath as something sharp pressed deeper into her calf. She curled up her toes, and pain shot through her feet.

Connor shifted and rubbed her shoulder. "Are ye all right, Katie?"

"Just…my feet really hurt."

"Can ye wait in here a bit longer? I'll make sure 'tis safe outside."

His muscles moved beneath her. Snuggle time was over. "I'll come, too."

"I'm thinkin' the men have gone, but I'll not take the chance. And as much as I enjoy yer company, my bladder tells me the two of us shall be needin' some time apart." He shifted his weight back and forth, pulling himself past her and out of the log.

Katie felt the loss of his warmth and not just physically. Lying flat on her stomach, she put her head on her arms, savoring the chance to stretch out, and waited, breathing in the breeze of fresh air until she finally heard Connor's voice. She recognized it, even though it was distant, but she couldn't understand what he said. She assumed he was on the phone. After a few moments of silence, she heard a noise and looked up to see him crouched down with an arm outstretched.

Taking hold of her wrists, he pulled as she squirmed and crawled—much less gracefully than he'd done—out of the log and into the lightening forest. Rotting leaves, mold, and underbrush covered the ground beneath them.

Kaitlyn balanced gingerly on her sore feet, still holding onto Connor's hands while she shifted her weight to find a way to stand that didn't shoot pain through her legs. "What time is it?"

"Nearly half-past five." The side of Connor's mouth lifted. "I'll need to apologize. Dinner didn't turn out quite the way I'd intended."

"Oh, really? Peril wasn't all part of your plan?" Kaitlyn tried for lighthearted tone, but her feet were killing her.

"Spendin' the night hidden in a maggot-infested log after being kidnapped and shot at, no, 'tisn't the evenin' I had planned at all." He tilted his head, looking at her face. "Ye didn't eat yer supper and must be starved."

"Not after you said the word maggot-infested." She wrinkled her nose.

He smiled. "I definitely didn't think we'd be spending the night together."

Looking down to hide her blush, she tugged at the muddy, ripped disaster that had been her favorite floral-print with ruffles at the knee. She glanced at Connor, who had a bit of dirt on his pants but otherwise looked as sharp and put together as he had last night. "How many girls can say they've been rescued from a castle tower?"

He nodded. "There's that."

"But, I'm definitely not a Bond girl."

Connor raised his eyebrows.

Kaitlyn combed fingers through her hair. "The action looks so much more exciting in the movies. You know, a daring rescue. Running from the bad guys. I'm not a very good adventure partner, and I could use a make-up crew." She limped awkwardly on one heel and the side of her other foot for a few steps to sit on the log, twisting around her leg to see what made her calves burn.

"I was terrified." She glanced toward him, speaking in a lowered voice. "I did everything wrong, and I made things worse. I didn't fight. I was so scared that I followed them like a brainwashed idiot, and I put you in danger, too." She focused on brushing off dirt and pulling wood splinters out of her calves and feet.

"Katie, yer feet." Connor crouched, resting one knee on the ground in front of her and lifted her leg.

His touch left behind tingles when he ran his hand across her bare skin. In spite of the throbbing pain in her feet, she couldn't help but be relieved she'd taken the time to shave her legs yesterday.

His fingers brushed over a raised bruise on her shin and his jaw tightened as he examined her swollen foot. He shifted closer and gently twisted around her leg to check out the back of her calf.

"It's not so bad, just a few scrapes."

"A few scrapes? Yer calves look like *drisheen*."

She frowned. He compared her legs to ground sheep intestines? Not the most flattering compliment.

He leaned to check her other leg. "I'll need tweezers to get out these splinters, and ointment, or ye'll have some infection. Yer feet are swollen. I'm just prayin' that ye've no broken bones."

In spite of the pain, Kaitlyn was hyper-aware of his touch and the effect it had on her senses. Heat spread under her skin, and her pulse sounded in her ears. With an effort, she pulled her mind from her daydreaming to their current situation. She lowered her leg from his hands and spoke seriously. "Connor, what do we do now?"

He pressed his lips tight. "First, we need to talk."

Their teasing and intimate moments were over. She

nodded her agreement.

He straightened from his crouch and brushed off his slacks before he turned to sit by her on the mossy log. He rested his elbows on his legs and concentrated on his hands hanging between his knees as he spoke. "Katie, what I've told ye about the pendant 'tis the truth, though I've not told ye everythin'." He took a breath. "Ye'll remember I told ye Seamus gave me the three knots when I was but fifteen. He told me they're the key to findin' the lost treasure of Angus O'Brien."

"I don't understand. A key?"

He shrugged. "Naturally, I assumed he was only tellin' me a legend, and I didn't believe anythin' of what he was sayin'. But he was so earnest that I agreed to take them, to keep them safe, and never let an enemy get the group of them. 'Twas three years before I met ye."

He tilted his head. "When I knew ye were leavin', Katie, I wanted to give somethin' special…somethin' important. I'd have given ye the moon if I could, but these pendants were the most valuable things I owned. Seamus hadn't said a word about them since the night he gave them to me, and I hoped he'd forgotten about them. Indeed, I never heard him mention them again. Then four days ago when I returned home from a mission—"

"Mission?"

"Aye, just hear me out, then. I returned home, and Seamus had sent me a letter by post. Worried for his life he was, and"—Connor cleared his throat—"he feared enemies knew of the relics. Enemies who'd stop at nothin' to obtain them."

The way he spoke, so matter-of-factly, frightened

her more than the story he told. She shivered. "But I don't understand. Who *are* they?"

"Last night, I sent a photo of yer friend from the road to my gaffer, Jack. He identified him as Robbie Lynch, a known associate of an extremist group—the R-IRA. Lynch's fingerprints were also on Seamus'ss gun that was discovered in the pond."

Kaitlyn opened her eyes wide then squinted. "IRA? Like terrorists? I don't..." She tipped her head. "How does a government employee have access to terrorist criminal records? How did the IRA find out about the pendants? How did Seamus know they were after him? And, why do you have a gun? What's that you said about returning from a 'mission'? I'm pretty sure you weren't spreading the good word or visiting the Alamo."

He cocked his head. "The Alamo?"

Ignoring the question, she narrowed her eyes. "Connor, what aren't you telling me?"

He turned, his body facing her, and put his hands on her shoulders. "Katie, for ye to trust me, I need ye to know a few things. But ye must understand how important 'tis ye not repeat what I'm tellin' ye. 'Tis the sort of secret that would get me killed. Do ye understand?"

Her chest tightened. "Yeah, of course."

"I'm an agent for G-2. Are ye familiar with what that means?"

"No." A sick feeling rose in her stomach.

"G-2 is Ireland's National Intelligence Agency. I work in the anti-terrorism division. 'Tis where Seamus worked, too."

Kaitlyn shook her head. This information was too

much. "Seamus was...you're...*spies*?"

"Katie, infiltratin' organizations such as the R-IRA and findin' information on them, 'tis what we're trained for. I'm not knowin' exactly how Seamus found out they were after the relics and the treasure, but he's known 'twas a possibility and prepared for it these eleven years when he gave me the relics to keep safe."

"So, you got the letter, realized Seamus had died, and hurried back to Tullybrae?"

He gave a sharp nod. "I saw yer picture in the paper wearin' the pendant at the funeral. 'Tis why yer room was torn apart, I'm sure. And why ye were kidnapped." He grimaced. "I placed ye in danger, Katie, and for that, I'm sorry."

Katie dropped her gaze, thinking. The story sounded ridiculous, but she believed it without a doubt. She realized all the pig-headed, arrogant things Connor had done since he arrived, he'd done to keep her safe. The way he'd quizzed Ian before they went anywhere, how mad he'd been when she'd left the property alone. All the overprotectiveness. Now, she understood his intention. "What about Aunt Tillie?" she asked. "With you gone, she could be in danger."

"I'm havin' the manor house watched. I made a few phone calls earlier—while I was..."

She smirked. "While you were executing a clandestine operation?"

He raised his eyebrows, his lips twitching. "Aye."

Katie leaned back and crossed an arm across her chest to stretch her shoulder. She would feel the effects of being smashed in that log for days, not to mention the aching muscles from rock climbing. "So, Secret Agent Connor Flynn, what do we do now?"

"Well then, Katie. We'll be needin' a plan. But first, we're goin' to church."

Chapter 20

At first, Kaitlyn refused Connor's offer to carry her, insisting her feet looked worse than they felt. But after a few yards of limping, unsuccessfully stifling her groans, and clinging to his arm, she sagged in relief when he finally crouched down, pulling her onto his back. She held onto his shoulders and tried not to focus on the way his hands gripped the backs of her thighs, or that her skirt rode up around her waist and her fanny probably hung out. Her feet dangled at his sides, jolting with pain as they bounced with each of his steps.

Connor, however, didn't even appear winded. He maintained a constant pace—a rather rapid one—and didn't stop to rest. Once they were close to the main road, he helped her find a comfortable place to hide and wait while he went to retrieve the car.

She sat on the mossy ground, leaning against a tree.

He handed her his phone and showed her how to type in his password to get into the contact list. "If I'm not back in half an hour, call Tillie." He held her hand around the phone and lifted a leaf out of her hair. His fingers curled around to cup the back of her head, pulling her closer and pressing a warm kiss on her forehead. "I don't like leavin' ye here. Not when ye can't walk. But I think if danger appears, 'twill be on the road."

Kaitlyn placed her hand on the side of his face,

worry for his safety pushing away the warm feeling left behind by his tender care. "Be careful, Connor."

He held her a moment longer, their gazes locked. He glanced at her lips and back to her eyes.

Kaitlyn's breath hitched.

He brushed a thumb across her cheek and stood. Taking out his gun, he turned back and winked, and then disappeared into the trees.

Kaitlyn strained her ears, but the only sounds in the forest came from birds. She wondered what kinds of animals lived in the Irish woods. To distract herself from pain and worry, she used Connor's phone to look up the information. She was relieved to learn she wouldn't find anything more dangerous than a fox or a deer. Apparently, no snakes lived in Ireland—that fact was good fortune indeed.

She shifted to elevate her feet, thinking about the things Connor said. So many questions buzzed in her mind, and she realized she knew nothing about the IRA—the Irish Republican Army. Hadn't they been involved in bombings years ago? Were they still a threat? She got out Connor's phone again and typed in her query, amazed with the connection speed. G-2 must make sure their agents had top-of-the-line technology.

Finding an article, she read the IRA declared a ceasefire in 1998 and had legitimate government representation with their own party—Sinn Fein. The Real Irish Republican Army, or R-IRA, was a splinter group made up of the hardliners, the ones who refused to back down from their fight for independence from Britain and unification for all of Ireland.

Her stomach turned cold. How could she and Connor possibly hope to evade a group that was still a threat to an entire government? Why were the relics so important, and how had Seamus fit into the whole thing?

A twig snapped, and Katie went rigid. She scooted around the tree, away from the noise as silently as she could, hoping whatever made the sound was just a fluffy little forest inhabitant. She looked at the time notation on the phone. Connor had been gone for over twenty minutes. She hoped he was checking his car for bombs. Would he think of doing that?

Another rustle behind the tree set her heart racing. Listening, she sat as still as she could. She let out a breath of relief and a small laugh when a deer stepped past her.

Hearing her, the animal bounded away.

Twenty-eight minutes.

Scenarios churned in Kaitlyn's mind. Had Connor been ambushed when he got to his car? Had the terrorists taken him? Or hurt him? Or worse? She scrolled through the contacts until she reached Tillie's name. But just as she held her finger above it, ready to connect, she heard a car's engine. She caught a glimpse of a silver vehicle between the trees, and her body melted with relief.

Connor kept the engine running and ran into the trees, scooping her up and carrying her back to set her in the car.

Sitting on his soft leather seats as the car hummed down the road, she handed him the phone. "I was worried. I almost called Aunt Tillie."

He glanced at her, one side of his lips rising. "I told ye I'd be fine. Though it warms my heart that ye'd worry for me." When they pulled up in front of the church, Connor opened her door.

She turned her legs to the side, putting her feet carefully on the ground. When Connor moved to lift her, Katie pushed away his hand. "My skirt's too short for you to carry me like that. Why don't I just wait here?"

"I'll not leave ye alone on the road, Katie." He pulled her forward gently, wrapping his arm around her back. "And he's expectin' us."

"Think of how this situation looks. We're here first thing in the morning. My dress is all ripped up and dirty. What will Father McKenna think?"

"He may think we're here to confess." Connor's lips twitched.

"I just don't want him—or anyone else—getting the wrong idea about where we've been or what we've been doing."

"Katie, I'd hope the people o' Tullybrae know me well enough to trust that I'd not keep a young lady out in the woods overnight, just because I wanted—" He snorted. "Well, actually, I'd not mind if yer Ian gets the wrong idea."

Before Kaitlyn had a chance for a witty retort, the door of the church opened.

Father McKenna, his black robes swishing around him, hurried down the path.

Kaitlyn had met the man a few times since she'd arrived: at the wake, the funeral, and mass. She assumed the priest was probably in his forties. His dark hair was short with just a few gray patches showing at the temples. He was boyish, happy, and friendly, making him unlike any priest she'd ever met before.

"Connor, glad I am to see ye. I thank ye for ringin'

163

me this mornin' to give me warning of yer visit, otherwise ye'd have caught me in my bath. And Kaitlyn." Father McKenna paused, studying the damage to her feet and legs. "Mercy, and aren't ye a sight? Well, come on inside. We'll get ye cleaned up."

Connor lifted her and pushed the car door closed with his foot.

Kaitlyn held her skirt balled tight with her free hand to keep it from gaping too low.

Connor followed the priest through the gate and up the path into the church. They walked across the threshold and back in time. The stone floors of the chapel were uneven, and the wooden pews smelled of lemon oil. In a small alcove of the stone wall hung a statue of Christ on the cross surrounded by candles, the wax hardened into ribbons on the wooden shelf where it had dripped.

"Here we are, then. Have a seat while I see about finding first-aid supplies." Father McKenna's voice echoed in the stone building.

Connor set her gently on a pew in the back of the chapel. "Don't worry yerself, Father. I'll have her back at the manor house in a few minutes, and Tillie will tend to her." He scooted into the hard wooden pew as well.

Kaitlyn pulled what was left of her skirt over her knees, gazing around at the beautiful stained glass windows. Feeling embarrassed about the state of her clothing, she resisted looking at either man.

Father McKenna sat in the pew in front of them, turning so his arm lay across the back of the bench. "Are ye alright, then, Kaitlyn? Connor told me the two of ye had quite a night."

She glanced toward Connor, wondering what she should or shouldn't say in front of the priest but couldn't read any warning in his expression. "We had quite an adventure, Father." Kaitlyn hoped she'd stayed vague enough not to give too much away and also not be rude.

Father McKenna turned to Connor. "I've the...I've what ye've come for."

"Ye can speak freely in front of Katie, Father."

The priest's eyebrows lifted the slightest bit as he glanced between them. "Very well, then." He reached into his robes and pulled out an envelope.

Connor tore it open and tipped it to pour out the relic. He glanced at the charm before handing it to Kaitlyn.

She turned over the knot in her hand, running her finger across the pattern and traced the line that formed the knot. It was larger than her pendant, nearly covering her entire palm. The edges of the knot design were rounded instead of pointed. She handed it back to Connor.

He returned it to the envelope and slid it into his inner jacket pocket. "I thank ye for keepin' it for me, Father."

"Of course. Unless there's somethin' else ye'd like to discuss, I'll leave ye to gettin' this young lady home to her aunt." He moved to stand but paused, turning back and placing his hand over Kaitlyn's on the back of his pew. "Kaitlyn, 'tis nearly twenty years that I've known Connor Flynn, and I'd tell ye, though ye'd search for a lifetime, ye'd not be findin' a more trustworthy man." He patted her hand and stood to shake Connor's hand. "I hope to see ye soon, boy-o.

Perhaps ye'll join Tillie at Mass on Sunday."

"If I'm able, Father."

"'Til then God bless ye and keep ye safe, Connor. And yerself as well, Kaitlyn."

Connor bent to pick her up, his gaze meeting hers.

For a second, she saw naked fear in his expression. He quickly hid it, but she shivered. Though they hadn't discussed it, the threat obviously hadn't disappeared. She knew Connor felt the added weight of keeping Seamus's secret and maintaining her safety.

Instead of holding onto her skirt, she put her hands on his cheeks, turned his face to hers, and touched their foreheads together, hoping he would draw strength from the faith she had in him. If anyone could figure out what to do, the person would be Connor.

Chapter 21

Kaitlyn leaned back in the seat as Connor closed the car door. She watched as he pulled out his phone, dialing and talking as he walked slowly around to the driver's side. As he slid into the car, she caught the tail end of his conversation.

"—we'll be arrivin' in about ten minutes… Aye, and some food. She's not eaten since yesterday mornin'…"

Kaitlyn waved her hand in front of him to get his attention. "Is that Aunt Tillie? Don't worry her."

Connor up held his finger, signaling for her to wait. "Sure, and I know it. See ye soon, Tillie." He disconnected the call.

She grimaced. "I was hoping we could just sneak in without Aunt Tillie knowing."

"Do ye think she hasn't been phonin' all night? Worried out of her mind, she was."

Kaitlyn's throat constricted as she thought of how concerned Aunt Tillie must have been. "What should we tell her, Connor?"

"The truth."

"But—"

"Tillie's heard worse news."

Kaitlyn realized Aunt Tillie must have known all along—known the truth about Connor and Seamus and their work for the government. She tried to remember, but couldn't think of any indication Uncle Seamus wasn't what he seemed. He'd traveled often, she knew. But Aunt Tillie had never acted like his occupation was dangerous or out of the ordinary. Kaitlyn was amazed and a little hurt her aunt had kept this secret from her. "She's heard worse because her husband worked in G-2?"

Connor nodded.

They turned into the Manor House drive, and he waved to the security guard at the gate. He pulled in front of the steps and hadn't even shut off the car before Aunt Tillie ran through the front doors. Connor climbed from the car and was pulled into a tight embrace. They spoke for a moment, and then he opened Katie's door and lifted her out.

Kaitlyn hoped they wouldn't see anyone else. She hated feeling so dependent and knew her appearance would attract attention.

"Oh, my dear." Aunt Tillie touched her fingertips to her mouth when she saw Kaitlyn's feet. "Straight up to her room, then. I've had Cook prepare breakfast for ye, and I'll tend to yer injuries right away."

Connor carried her up the stairs and into her room, setting her into a soft chair next to a table set with a tray of porridge and sweet bread.

Aunt Tillie bustled in right behind them, pouring Kaitlyn a cup of tea. "Ye'll stay and have some breakfast then, Connor? Or at least a cuppa?"

Frowning, Connor looked at the fire. He blinked before he looked at Aunt Tillie. "I've matters that need seein' to." His gaze moved to Kaitlyn, traveling over her ruined dress and down to her swollen feet and cracked toenails. "Take care of Katie." He grabbed a slice of bread and hurried out of the room.

Kaitlyn felt a little hurt that he hadn't said good-bye, or that he hadn't discussed any plans with her, but those thoughts didn't last long. The pain in her feet drove any other worries from her mind.

When Kaitlyn had eaten as much breakfast as she could, Aunt Tillie ran a hot bath. Kaitlyn leaned on her aunt, and on the furniture, making her way carefully into the bathroom where she pulled off the muddy torn dress and sank beneath the steaming water, gasping as it stung her feet. After washing her hair, she only allowed herself the indulgence of soaking for a few minutes longer since Aunt Tillie waited. She wrapped in a thick towel and limped to the wardrobe where her aunt helped her slide a nightgown over her head and instructed her to lie down on her stomach.

Tillie sat on the bed next to her, with a pair of tweezers, and started working the splinters out of her legs. "Well, my dear, the good news is yer legs don't look quite as bad now that ye've cleaned up. Though they'll still be needin' a bit o' work to keep away the infection."

At the shooting pain, Kaitlyn sucked in a breath. "Thanks, Aunt Tillie."

"I am so sorry ye became involved in this mess. 'Tis a fearful night ye had."

Kaitlyn winced at the sting as Aunt Tillie tugged a little too hard on a splinter. "Connor told me about him and Uncle Seamus. I mean, he told me what kind of work they do. How did you stand the strain for so long? Your husband away on dangerous missions? And all the secrets?"

"Seamus, he'd been retired for years, but I'll tell

ye, I'd a difficult time with his career at the beginning of our marriage. 'Twasn't right for a husband to keep secrets from his wife, I thought. But now I know 'twas for my safety…and his. I'd not heard about the relics or the treasure until today when Connor told me, and 'tis easy to see now why Seamus chose to keep it hidden." Tillie wiped the towel over Kaitlyn's legs then helped her stand and limp to the bench at the foot of the bed.

"So, what will happen?" Kaitlyn asked as Aunt Tillie dabbed cool ointment onto her scrapes. "Are we safe here?"

"I don't think we've seen the end of this problem, my dear." Tillie pinched the skin at her throat and pursed her lips. "But I do know of no one on this earth I trust with my life, and that of my only niece, more than Connor. He'll be formulatin' a plan as we speak, and yer safety and mine are his top priority." Aunt Tillie walked into the bathroom and returned with a comb and a drink of water. She took a bottle of pills out of her pocket, poured two into her palm, and handed them to Kaitlyn with the glass. "Now, take these, then. They'll ease yer pain and help ye sleep, so they will."

Kaitlyn obeyed. The ointment was already soothing her legs.

Tillie sat next to her and began pulling the comb through Kaitlyn's wet, matted hair.

But the action was far from soothing. Kaitlyn turned over what she'd learned in the last few hours. Feeling scared and betrayed, her entire perspective on her family and Connor shifted around until she hardly recognized them. Did she even know Connor at all? If he was indeed a spy, could his skills keep her and Aunt Tillie safe?

****

"A shoe? Ye brought me her bloody shoe?"

Robbie Lynch watched as his gaffer held the shoe, letting it dangle off his finger by one sparkling strap. The broken heel attached by a bit of silver patent leather flopped unnaturally.

"What, pray tell, am I supposed to do with this?" He clenched the shoe in his hand and threw it hard against the wall behind him.

Lynch stared at the scrape it left in the peeling paint of the dingy apartment. He took in a calming breath before turning back toward the man who called the shots in this operation. He'd been surprised the first time he'd met the gaffer. Not only by his age, but believing this naive-looking person was universally feared and ranked so highly in their organization was difficult. Lynch held his tongue, though. He'd been warned not to underestimate the man.

"I asked ye to do a simple task—get her necklace and keep her until I got there." The gaffer paced four steps before turning on the worn carpet. "Yer telling me she climbed out the window? She was hanging over the cliff? Ye call that watching her?"

Lynch rubbed his cramping shoulder muscles, careful not to bump his fresh stitches. He gritted his teeth. "I told ye, babysitting's not in my job description."

"Aye, and ye could have used yer other skills to get rid of Flynn. But now we're stuck with the man." He stopped pacing and stood with his hands on his hips. "We need him to deliver the treasure to us. And though I hate working with him, the people I report to trust he'll do what he says."

"Why not just go in and take the damn relics?" Lynch cracked his knuckles. The idea of giving Connor Flynn a little payback for all the trouble he'd caused last night was just too tempting. Lynch hadn't particularly enjoyed the ribbing from his partners and the reprimands from his superiors for allowing the escape. Not to mention Flynn was responsible for the bullet that scraped his shoulder, left a tear in his favorite jacket, and necessitated a visit to a disgusting basement clinic where a person he hoped had a modicum of medical training stitched him up with no anesthesia.

"The plan works out better for all of us this way. We don't have to go on a treasure hunt with the *guarda* knowing our location, and Flynn keeps his enemies away from his home."

"What's to keep him from takin' the treasure and runnin', then?" *That's what I'd do.* The gaffer's condescending look made Lynch grind his teeth.

"A pretty blonde and an old lady. People like Flynn are easy to manipulate once ye know their weakness. He's promised to deliver the treasure by tomorrow noon."

Lynch scowled. "Why so long? I can't believe 'twill take an entire day for him to get it."

"That's the agreement. I wasn't the one who made the deal. I assume he's buyin' time to get security measures in place for the ladies. No matter, we'll get what we want. And afterward, ye'll make sure Flynn won't be around to tell his story."

Lynch crossed his arms, puffing out his chest. "Perfect."

****

Connor paced around his room and finally sat at his desk. He'd left Kaitlyn in good hands. Tillie would know how to take care of her cuts. Though she'd tried to downplay her injuries, he had seen in her eyes how badly her feet hurt. They were swollen and scraped, and ugly purple bruises grew on them and on her legs. Her toenails were cracked and bloody. He rubbed the back of his neck, guilt sinking his stomach for the hundredth time since last night. *Why had he let her out of his sight at the pub?*

He pulled out of his jacket pocket the envelope Father McKenna gave him and took Katie's necklace from the top drawer. For a moment, he studied both of the knots, hoping for some new insight before returning them to the envelope and then back into his pocket. But none came. After standing, he paced in front of the fireplace, laying the foundation of his plan. His contact gave him until noon tomorrow. That meant he had less than twenty-four hours, not only to find the treasure but to set an operation in place to thwart his enemies' plans and hopefully capture key members of the R-IRA. Anxiety balled in his stomach. He'd planned intricate operations in less time than that. But this time, the risks involved people he loved. He couldn't fail.

As for now, too many variables existed to set anything in motion. The first step was obvious, though. He needed to retrieve the last relic from its hiding place.

Connor showered and changed his clothes. He noticed the backs of his legs had a few scratches, but nothing like the hash that marked Kaitlyn's calves. He walked down the back stairs, through the kitchen, grabbing a battery-operated torch before he headed outside and around to the side of the Manor House.

If he used this access instead of the one in the dining room, Connor had a better chance of remaining unseen. Since he didn't have the luxury of waiting for the obscurity of darkness, he surveyed the area carefully before pushing aside the tendrils of ivy that covered the wall. Years had passed since he'd looked for the hidden door. Priest's holes were rare in Ireland, and Uncle Seamus had theorized this particular passageway was built for the lord's family to escape in case the Manor House was threatened, not to hide illegal clergy.

Connor pulled aside vines of ivy which stuck like they'd been glued to the old stones, prodding different bricks until he found a small lever. After one more quick look around, he pressed the lever and heaved against the wall. It budged, but the old hinges were rusty. Pushing his shoulder into the ivy, he grunted as the stone door finally moved. A waft of cold, dank air emerged as the gap between the door and the wall grew. Finally, when the opening was large enough, he flicked on his light and, turning sideways, he slipped into the dark tunnel.

The passage held the smell of stale air and the damp feel of being underground. Connor closed the heavy door most of the way, leaving only a small gap. He shined his light down the short hallway to where it opened into a larger room. Wooden benches had been built against the walls beneath small alcoves which originally held candles. On the far side, a narrow, steep staircase wound up to the floor above, where the other secret door was hidden in the mantle of the dining room's fireplace. Connor stood still and listened for a short minute to the clank of dishes and murmurs of lunchtime conversation overhead.

He stepped up onto one of the old benches and reached into the alcove above it. Finding the right brick, he wiggled it back and forth with his fingertips until he pulled it free. He shined the light into the recess and pulled out a small wooden rectangle, remembering the first time he'd held this box in the underground passage all those years ago. Opening the lid, he ensured the last relic was there, as well as the slip of paper that was apparently his only clue to using the knots. He would need to examine it in better light. He replaced the stone and had just stepped off the bench when out of the corner of his eye, he saw a shadow cross in front of the gap he'd left open in the Manor House wall.

Connor clicked off his torch and hurried to the opening, peering through, and then pushed open the door and slipped outside. He looked around and saw nobody. Maybe the shadow had just been a cloud moving in front of the sun. He slid the box into his pocket. Pulling the door into place, he arranged the ivy to conceal the entrance and started back to the kitchen.

When he stepped around the corner, he heard a voice calling his name.

Mrs. Wilkie and the man he'd seen her with the night before at the pub were walking toward him. They were coming from the direction of the putting green. They moved too slowly to have passed in front of the secret door. A conversation with them would be more irritating than necessary. Before he searched for the treasure, he was anxious to check on Katie. Connor swallowed his frustration and put on his "welcoming the guests" face.

"Top o' the mornin', Connor." Mrs. Wilkie gave a bright smile.

Would tourists ever get tired of saying that? "And the rest of the day to yerself," he responded automatically, his smile tightening.

"Connor, I'd like you to meet my husband, Stanley Wilkie. Sugar, this gentleman is Connor. He's a relative of Tillie's. He's been staying at the manor for a few days, paying his respects, but this chance is the first I've had to introduce the two of y'all."

The men shook hands and sized up one another. Stanley Wilkie was balding, overweight, and sunburned. *How does one even get a sunburn in Ireland?* His face reminded Connor of a Bassett hound with jowls that shook when he spoke. The man stood with his head leaned back slightly if he was looking down his nose at Connor, who was at least a foot taller.

Stanley squinted. "You missed the funeral by a few weeks. Young people these days don't have the same sense of duty as the older generation. Ya just showing up now to see if you have an inheritance check?"

Connor blinked. A flash of anger heated his face. He opened and closed his mouth, attempting to form an answer.

"Oh, Sugar. He probably just couldn't get away. Am I right, Connor?" Mrs. Wilkie slipped her hand into the bend of her husband's elbow, her neon pink fingernails poking out of the fleshy rolls of Stanley's arm. "You know, not everyone can pick up and leave at a moment's notice. Where do you work, Connor?"

"Dublin."

"Dublin!" Stanley snorted. "The city's not even three hours away. I've driven back and forth from

Dublin *twice* this week."

Connor could hear Tillie's voice in his head, *Treat the guests with all kindness, for 'tis their special vacation to the Emerald Isle, after all.* "What line of work are ye in, Mr. Wilkie?" He forced his voice to remain pleasant.

"The import-export business, son. Nothing like good, old-fashioned hard work. My generation, we're not afraid of getting our hands dirty." He squinted again, looking Connor over. "Let me guess. You work in retail. Men's clothing? Am I right?"

"And ye certainly know how to read people, Mr. Wilkie," Connor said.

"Shrewd, boy. Shrewd is what you have to be in the business world, or you'll get eaten alive."

Mrs. Wilkie looked at her husband with adoration written all over her face. She tugged on his arm. "Come on, Sugar. I'm ready for lunch, aren't you?"

"I thank ye for yer excellent advice, then. I'll not detain ye from yer meal this fine day." Connor shook both of their hands again, making a note to check on whether the Wilkies were guests at the manor house when Seamus was killed.

Again, Mrs. Wilkie pulled her husband's pudgy arm, and they started toward the dining room. Mr. Wilkie expounded the virtues of hard work and the laziness of the younger generation until they were out of earshot.

Connor turned in the other direction, back around the Manor House to the front entrance—not that any place was far enough away from the Wilkies. He raised a hand in greeting as he passed Fergus weeding in Aunt Tillie's roses then strode through the entrance hall and took the steps two at a time, not wanting to risk having to chat with anyone else. When he got to Kaitlyn's room, he knocked softly.

Tillie opened the door.

Connor put his hand on Tillie's shoulder and looked past her to Katie. "Is she all right, then?"

Tillie leaned close. "Aye, I've given her somethin' to put her right to sleep." She glanced back at the bed. "I've things that need attendin'. Make sure to let her get some rest." She opened the door wide.

Connor stepped inside. His gaze moved past her to where Katie sat combing out her hair. The window behind her cast a warm glow, shining on her wet hair and illuminating soft curves where her nightgown clung. He itched to touch her. Heat expanded in his chest, and his heart beat a hard rhythm.

Tillie excused herself. She picked up a towel from the bed, folded it then carried it and the breakfast tray out of the room.

Connor sat on the bench next to Katie, turning her shoulders so she faced away. He took the comb. "Here, let me have a go with that." Gently, he pulled the comb through her hair. His fingers brushed against the heat of her neck. He swallowed. "And are ye feelin' better, now?"

"Just sleepy. I don't know what Aunt Tillie gave me, but I can hardly keep my eyes open."

He set a section of smooth hair over her shoulder, fascinated as he watched it spring into silky curls and started on the next.

"Connor, will we be okay, now? I mean these guys got in here once before. I just…"

"I'll not let anyone harm ye, Katie. Yer safe."

Connor lifted her hair, running the comb through it, and watching the small curls form around her hair line and the nape of her neck as they dried.

"That feels good," Katie's words slurred. She leaned back against his chest and yawned.

Connor's arms wrapped around her as if they had a mind of their own. He rubbed the smooth skin of her arms. He held her as her body relaxed against his and wondered if she could feel his heart thundering.

Her head nodded toward her chest, and she snapped it back up. "Connor, don't do anything dangerous."

"Whist, Katie."

She yawned again. "Promise me? I don't want you to get hurt."

He brushed his face against her damp hair, inhaling the fresh scent, hoping to imprint it in his mind along with the feel of her in his arms He didn't know what the next twenty-four hours would bring, but he couldn't imagine the men he was dealing with were the type to simply thank him for the treasure and leave him to be on his merry way. He hoped the trap would work, but if not, he hopefully would have kept danger from the two people he cared most about. A pang of regret lodged somewhere around his diaphragm as he forced his mind to the mission he needed to accomplish. "Come. 'Tis to bed with ye, then." He lifted Katie and carried her to the bed, sliding the sheets over her body.

Her eyes closed, and her breathing deepened. "Will you stay until I'm asleep?" she murmured.

"Aye." He brushed his fingers over her cheek followed by a soft kiss. That promise was one he could keep.

Chapter 22

Twenty minutes later, Connor spread out the three relics on his desk. Each was shaped in a different pattern, though they were formed from the same golden brass. He moved them around, turning them to form different patterns or pictures. Did they contain a map of the grounds? Or a secret message? Did they form an image?

Finally, he turned his attention to the roll of parchment he'd found in the box. The note was old and brittle. When he unrolled it, he saw irregular blotted lettering, most likely made by a fountain pen. Though the writing had faded and the ink had feathered, he could still read the words:

Within the hated wood on which daily I trod
The three form the key
Through the symbol of anchor and rod

Connor read the lines dozens of times. He assumed "the three" referred to the three knots. But what was "the symbol of anchor and rod"? Did the knots make a picture of a fish? Or a ship? Or a fishing pole?

"Wood on which daily I trod." That line could refer to almost anything. All the floors in the manor house were wooden. Connor doubted they were original to Angus's time. They'd surely been replaced. And why *hated* wood? Where did Angus have to walk every day that he hated?

Connor stood and paced back and forth across his room, thinking of what he knew about Lord Angus O'Brien. Obviously, the Lord had spent most of his time in the Great Hall where he'd attended to his court and oversaw the running of his estate. Where else would Lord Angus have walked daily? The dining room? His private chambers? Which of those places had the lord despised enough to call it "hated"? When Connor showed the riddle to Tillie, she'd not had any insight either.

Connor slid the relics into his pocket. Just thinking about it was getting him nowhere. He hurried out of his room and down the hall to stand on the landing overlooking the great entry hall. His gaze searched for any sort of pattern on the floor or the wooden beams in the walls and high ceiling that might relate to the knots.

He walked down the steps slowly, looking at each board as he went. Searching for what, he didn't know. Would a small symbol be carved into the floor? Or did the clue relate to the furniture? Most of the antique furniture had been preserved throughout the manor but not all. In the great hall alone were chairs, side board tables, and two enormous mantelpieces.

Connor walked around the circumference of the room, focusing on the floor boards, looking for anything that might be a clue.

Although most of the guests were out on day-excursions, or taking advantage of the fine weather, the few remaining people gave him funny looks, especially when he moved the large leather chairs and rolled up a large carpet. He found nothing.

Discouraged, he re-positioned the chairs and stood in front of Lord Angus's statue, looking into the cruel face. *What have I missed? What is it I'm not seein'?*

Next, Connor moved into the dining room. A few hours still remained before dinner would be served. He studied the floors closely and from a distance, moving tables and chairs then examining every inch of an antique cabinet. None of these places seemed a likely spot to hide a treasure. Was he to believe that it was just under a floor board? How could the answer possibly be that easy? And if 'twas the case, how had the treasure not been discovered through the years of remodeling? He'd just stood from inspecting the mantel when he turned and saw Ian Kerry watching him.

Ian's eyes were cold. "I was worried when Kaitlyn missed her lesson this mornin'. When I rang her room and received no answer, I asked Tillie to check on her, but she assured me Kaitlyn was fine. Her lack of response leads me to believe that perhaps she'd not returned from her night out with her *old dear friend*."

Connor pushed his fingers through his hair. He didn't have time for this. "What are ye accusin' me of, then? Spendin' time with Katie?"

"*Nil.* 'Tis takin' advantage of her that I'd be accusin' ye of." Ian's nostrils flared.

"I'd not force her to do anythin' she didn't want to. She's a woman grown, is Katie. And she's able to make her own decisions." Connor tucked a chair beneath a table and turned, dismissing the tennis player.

"Kaitlyn was happy until ye came. She and I were—" Ian stopped talking and glanced toward a doorway.

Tillie entered the room and greeted both of them before turning to Ian. "If ye'll excuse us, Ian, I've some matters to discuss with Connor."

Ian's lips tightened. He shot a cold look at Connor before he turned and left the room without a word.

Tillie didn't seem to notice any discomfort. "And have ye found anythin', then?"

Connor shook his head, raking his fingers through his hair. "I was just about to ask ye for the key to search yer rooms. And then Seamus'soffice. But truthfully, Tillie, 'tis just like I told ye a few hours ago. I've no idea what I'm lookin' for."

"If anyone will solve the riddle, 'tis my Connor. I've faith in ye." Tillie pulled on his arm. "But ye can't be workin' on an empty stomach. Ye need to eat something besides the small slice of sweet bread ye had this morning." She led him into the kitchen for a sandwich.

After eating quickly, Connor kissed Tillie on the head and strode back through the great hall and up the stairs. Opening the door, he stepped into the lord of the manor's private chambers. He glanced around the small parlor Tillie used as an office. What furniture would have been here since the time of Lord Angus? He surveyed the entire floor, inch by inch. He examined all the furniture and moved into the bedroom.

The bed—that huge thing was definitely the same. Seamus and Tillie's bed was a massive antique with carved wooden posts at each corner that held up a tapestry canopy. Connor used his flashlight to scrutinize the floor beneath the bed, the bed posts, the carvings on the head and footboards then turned his attention to the remainder of the bedroom furniture. He ran his hands over the carvings in the doors of the wardrobe where Seamus'ss shirts still hung in an orderly row. *What would Seamus do? How would he tackle this problem?*

He'd be systematic about the process. He'd not be impulsive but analytical.

Connor got down on his knees and shined his light under the wardrobe, sliding his hand beneath it to feel the wood for any abnormalities. He sat back on his heels, letting out a breath. Aside from Seamus's office, where else would Lord Angus have "trod daily"? The grounds were extensive.

He left Tillie's room and walked slowly down the stairs. He could hear voices coming from the dining room, and his heart sank when he realized how late the hour had become. He'd leave Seamus'ss office for later and use the remaining daylight to search outside. Connor stopped to examine the wooden front doors and door frame then he walked through the main entrance and out onto the grounds.

For a moment, he stood on the front steps, scanning the area, muttering the rhyme. *"Within the hated wood on which daily I trod."* Could the "wood" mean the forest? If the treasure was buried in the forest, Connor figured his chances of finding it were pretty slim. His instinct told him the lord would keep it close by. But he'd searched the Manor House. A ball of fear grew in his stomach. He breathed deeply in an attempt to ignore it, but 'twas nearly seven o'clock, and he only had until noon tomorrow.

Chapter 23

Kaitlyn woke slowly. "Connor?" Darkness had fallen, and she looked around for the clock. *How long did I sleep?* Her head felt like it was stuffed with cotton. She rolled over, intending to drift off again when all at the same time, she registered the pain in her feet, her growling stomach, and the knowledge the threat of danger remained—Connor!

Had he figured out something? Had he called the police? Sitting bolt upright, she turned on her lamp. The time was past eleven o'clock. No wonder she was starving. She set her feet on the ground, tentatively putting weight on them. She could stand. She stepped into her slippers and found that walking wasn't as painful as she'd dreaded.

Hurriedly, she dressed in loose slacks and a sweater and, supporting herself against the wall, limped gingerly down the hallway. The manor house was quiet. That was a good sign. Had Connor figured out everything? Had the police arrested the terrorists? She walked through the silent house, down the stairs, and into the kitchen, cutting herself a large slice of soda bread. She thought she saw a shadow pass in front of the door and whipped around. "Hello?" she called.

But she received no answer. Her heart raced as she walked back through the dining room. Had the terrorists come to the manor house? She walked with no noise, searching, but saw nobody.

As she passed through the great hall, she heard a sound and noticed a bar of light beneath Seamus's office door. She was acting like a stupid girl from a horror film, going toward the light. But if danger was present, she needed to know and to warn Connor. She limped as softly as she could to Seamus's office, pushing open the door.

Inside, Connor sat in Seamus's chair, surrounded by open files and books. Papers covered the desk and spilled onto the floor. Connor pulled another stack of files out of Seamus's drawer. He dumped it on the desk before opening the top folder, scanning each paper inside, and then pushing it aside and opening the next one. His face was pale, and lines had formed around his mouth.

Kaitlyn paused, worrying as she took in his appearance. "Connor."

He started, his head whipping toward her. But instead of looking pleased to see her, he sank back into the chair and rubbed his eyes.

"Are you all right?" she asked.

"No, Katie. I'm afraid I've failed ye."

"What's wrong? What are you looking for?" She stepped into the room.

"Lord Angus's treasure. But I've searched the house and grounds, and I've found nothin'." Dark circles shadowed under his eyes.

"Have you even slept today? Or eaten? We can look for the treasure later. I'll help you clean up this mess tomorrow." She stepped closer, sliding her hand under his arm and tugging. "Come on. You need a break."

"Katie, ye don't understand. I've not the time to rest. I must deliver the treasure tomorrow by noon."

"Deliver the treasure to whom?" Kaitlyn squinted for a few moments before opening her eyes wide, a cold tendril of worry moving through her as she realized the implication behind his words. Connor had made a deal. He'd promised to hand over the treasure in exchange for what? Tillie's and her own safety? Probably. Why had he taken this upon himself? The responsibility was more than one person could do alone. "Connor, people have been searching for this treasure for centuries. What made you think you could find it in one day?"

Connor pulled a small box out of his coat pocket. It was about the size of a smart-phone. He extended it.

She set down her slice of bread before taking and examining it. The wooden box was stained dark with old-fashioned hinges. She opened the lid and found what must be all three relics resting inside. One by one, she pulled them out, examining each, and then set them on an empty spot on the desk, next to Seamus's computer. She glanced at Connor and arched an eyebrow.

He looked back at the box, nodding for her to continue.

Kaitlyn tipped the box toward her and reached her fingers inside, pulling out a small cigarette-sized roll of parchment, and unscrolled it carefully on the desk. She read it a few times before looking at Connor. "What does this mean?"

Connor rubbed his palm over the back of his neck. "I believe 'tis a clue to discoverin' the treasure, but I don't understand it. I've run out of ideas."

She re-read the note. "What have you tried?"

"I've searched every inch of the wooden floor in the manor house. Wherever I'd expect that Lord Angus would have trodden. The great hall, the lord's private chambers, the dining room…"

"Here in the office?" She glanced around, wondering if a treasure chest was hidden somewhere among the bookshelves and files.

"Aye. And I searched the forest until 'twas too dark."

"The 'wood.' That was smart." Katie studied the parchment as she spoke. "What does this mean, 'the three form the key. Through the symbol of anchor and rod'?"

"I assumed the relics combined to form a symbol, or a picture, or a message, or even a map. I've not found anything there, either."

"Maybe the term is something Lord Angus and his contemporaries would have understood." Kaitlyn studied the pendants. "May I use this computer?"

Nodding, Connor turned on the computer then stood.

Kaitlyn limped around the table to sit in the desk chair he'd vacated.

He leaned his forearms on the back of the chair.

She had a hard time concentrating on the screen with his hands so close to her hair again. *Is anything more blissful than having a man combing your hair?* Kaitlyn did a search for Celtic knots, clicking on page after page, reading about the various knots, and matching the relics to the examples she found.

After watching for a few minutes, Connor turned back to the stack of papers. "I'll keep lookin' through Seamus's files, then." He sat in a chair on the other side of the desk.

Kaitlyn nodded and continued clicking and reading. A few minutes later, she read something that made her heart leap. "Connor, I found something."

He leaned over her shoulder, looking at the computer screen.

His cheek was so close to hers that she could feel his heat. She only had to turn her face the slightest bit, and they'd be a breath apart. Katie inhaled, pushing the thought out of her mind, and read.

The Sailor's knot is known as the lover's knot, in part, because it is actually two or more separate knots intertwined. Celtic sailors often used this knot in their artwork intended for their sweethearts.

Kaitlyn picked up the relics, and after a few tries, she attached the three together in a Sailor's knot, with two side by side and the other holding them together.

Connor took the object from her, turning it over in his hands, and then looked up. The smallest light of hope lit his eyes. "Ye figured it out, Katie. The key. Now, what do we do with it?"

"Let's go over the wood floors again. Maybe now that we've got this, we'll know what we're looking for when we see it."

The two left Seamus's office, locking the door behind them, and stepped into the great hall. Aunt Tillie kept a few sconces burning in the main hall during the night.

Kaitlyn leaned heavily against the doorframe, waiting for her vision to adjust to the soft light.

Connor held the Sailor's knot and walked around the perimeter of the room.

Concentrating on the wooden floor in the dim light,

Kaitlyn limped behind him. She stopped when her feet hurt too badly and sat on the stairs. Over and over, Kaitlyn read the lines on the parchment roll. " 'The hated wood.' Why does he call it the *hated* wood?" she muttered to herself.

She stood and limped toward the statue, studying Angus's face as if the answer would be written there. What would cause Lord Angus to hate walking on…? Kaitlyn froze, staring up at the statue. *"Within the hated wood on which daily I trod."* *Of course.* She jolted as the answer hit. Why hadn't she thought of it before? "Connor." Her voice echoed through the hall.

He rushed to her side, putting his arm around her shoulder. "Are ye alright? Are yer feet hurtin'?"

Her mind still reeling, Katie shook her head. "I know where Lord Angus hid his treasure."

Chapter 24

Kaitlyn felt Connor's gaze on her as she walked to the figure of Lord Angus. She knelt on the floor, reaching into the shadowed space beneath the statue and running her hand over the lord's leg.

"Katie, 'tis made of bronze, not wood." Connor squatted beside her.

Her heart tripped when she found what she was looking for, a small opening in the space behind Lord Angus's knee. She turned to Connor. "Lord Angus had a wooden leg. Get it? That's why it's the *hated* wood. Nobody likes having a wooden leg. Here, hand me the key." She looked at Connor who watched her with raised eyebrows. "The Sailor's Knot. What if it's an actual key? And a gap is here, a slit, hidden in the wrinkles of his pants. I think it will just fit…"

Connor knelt next to her and offered the key.

Kaitlyn studied it, turning it around until she thought the fit was right, and then carefully she slid the key into the crack. A click sounded before Lord Angus's leg disengaged, fell off, and hit the floor with a hollow clunk. A giddy feeling grew inside. She turned to Connor, expecting to see him staring at the leg lying on the floor, but his gaze was fixed on her.

"How did ye know, Katie?"

"The books. Remember those books that—" Her words were cut off when Connor pulled her close and wrapped her in a crushing embrace. He breathed heavily into her hair, and she twisted and scooted closer, so she could sit more comfortably in his arms.

Connor leaned back and held her face in his hands, and the tension that had tightened the skin around his eyes relaxed. "Ye did it, Katie." His gaze dropped for a moment to her lips.

A delicious ache started in her chest. She parted her lips and closed her eyes, but instead of Connor's mouth pressing on hers, she felt his fingers gently running down the sides of her neck until he placed his hands on her shoulders. She opened her eyes and saw his teasing smile.

"I told ye I'd not kiss ye until ye asked me to."

Katie sat up quickly. She pretended to frown at Connor's teasing but couldn't help the smile that slipped onto her face. Nonetheless, the romantic mood was ruined. Back to the business at hand. She folded her arms. "Well, should we see what the treasure is? I didn't hear any diamonds or gold doubloons spill out."

Connor picked up the heavy leg, holding onto Lord Angus's skinny ankle above the buckled shoe as he examined the interior of the statue's calf. He reached a hand inside and pulled out a folded piece of paper.

"Oh no." Kaitlyn groaned. "Please say it's not another clue." She couldn't imagine they could solve a new riddle before tomorrow at noon.

Connor unfolded it and studied the paper before turning it toward her.

No words were written, only numbers. Looking closer, she saw the numbers were divided into two sets. The first followed by an N and the second by a W. "What is this?"

"GPS coordinates," Connor said. "In Seamus'ss handwritin'. He's moved the treasure."

Kaitlyn sagged, a little disappointed at not having actually found a stash of jewels or gold. "So, what do we do now?"

"We'll need a bit more time on the computer to figure out this location. 'Twon't be hard to find. But first, I think Lord Angus might be wantin' his leg back." He stood and pulled her up with him. Connor held the heavy leg, while Kaitlyn guided it into position. When they lifted it into place, a click sounded, and the key fell out. The knots separated when they hit the floor, and she picked up the three items, handing them to Connor.

He pulled the box out of his jacket pocket and set them inside then extended it. "Keep them, Katie. Ye were the one who discovered how they worked. I'm truly proud of ye."

Her face flushed with pleasure, glad she could help ease his worry.

Sliding an arm around her waist, he pressed her against him. He lifted her chin, holding her gaze as he leaned his face closer.

Kaitlyn's pulse sped.

Connor traced a finger around her lips. He held the back of her head.

She felt tingles where he touched her. His whiskers scratched as his lips swept across her cheek. Turning her face slightly toward him, she sighed, craving the feel of his mouth on hers.

"Was there somethin' ye wanted to ask me, Katie?" he murmured.

She pulled back, seeing the smirk on his face that

didn't fully hide the smoldering in his dark eyes. "Connor. I really want you to kiss me." Kaitlyn had the satisfaction of seeing his eyes widen.

He blinked before his cocky smile returned. "Do ye now?" Cupping her chin, he brushed his lips across hers before he pushed his hand into her hair and covered her mouth with his.

Heat spread under her skin, and she wrapped her arms around his neck.

Connor drew back.

His blue eyes had darkened even further, and she felt his warm breath.

He leaned his forehead against hers. "I'd like to be continuin' this later if ye don't mind." He drew a breath and rubbed a thumb over her bottom lip. "When I can take my time about it." He winked and dropped his hands to hers, leading her toward the stairs. "And are ye too tired to do a bit more research, then? A few minutes on my laptop, and I hope we'll know what Seamus was thinkin'. Where he wanted us to go. We should be formulatin' a plan."

Kaitlyn and Connor walked up the stairs, and she thought how right being with him felt. His hand was warm and strong around hers. His kiss brought back fluttery teenage feelings and aroused new, deeper ones. She had her Connor back, and things were right again. She was in love with him. She always had been, and now instead of growing up and moving on, her feelings were even stronger. But a small thought kept sliding into her mind, chasing away the feeling of contentment she held onto so strongly. Why had Connor broken off contact all those years ago? Of course, she was naïve to believe the estrangement wouldn't happen again. A heaviness grew in her chest, and her step faltered. As much as she wanted to be with him, she was afraid he didn't reciprocate her feelings.

Connor stopped next to her. "Are ye all right, Katie? 'Tis yer feet hurtin' ye again?"

The concern in his voice just made the lump in her throat grow. "I'm okay." She forced a cheerful tone to her voice, though she couldn't meet his gaze.

"And shall I carry ye, then?" He shifted, lowering his shoulder, as he prepared to lift her.

"No." She tightened her grip on his hand. "I don't want you to."

Connor's eyebrows drew together. But he didn't say anything. He straightened and led her the rest of the way to his room. He opened the door and pulled a chair next to his at the desk holding his laptop. Once she sat, he sat beside her. Spreading out the folded paper on the desk, he began typing.

In a short time, they examined at a 3D satellite map of Ireland, and Connor located the position that matched the GPS coordinates. He enlarged the landscape, studying it. "The area's rural and wooded. About ten miles north of the city of Ennis." He zoomed in, and they both leaned toward the screen searching for anything that would indicate why Seamus had chosen this spot. Connor scrolled around the area slowly and found a small clearing.

"Ah." Connor leaned back in his chair. "I should have known. Seamus always had a fascination for Druids and their ceremonies."

Kaitlyn looked closer at the screen. She didn't see anything but a few rocks in the clearing. "What do you mean?"

"'Tis a Stone Circle. A Druid's Ring." Connor tapped the screen, indicating the standing stones barely visible between the trees.

The configuration didn't look quite symmetrical, and areas of the circle appeared to be missing. But seeing the structure in the computer image was hard, and Connor zoomed in as far as he could without losing resolution. "So, what's the plan, then?" Kaitlyn asked.

"Ye keep this." Connor folded the paper again and handed it to her. He pulled out another piece of paper and spent a few moments scrolling around on the map before he wrote down coordinates and pocketed his own copy.

Kaitlyn looked at Connor who still studied the map on the screen. She slid the folded paper into her pocket next to the box with the relics and stood, wincing at the pain in her feet. "I guess I better get to sleep." She started limping to the door when she felt Connor's hand on her arm.

"I'll walk ye to yer room."

"It's okay. I can make it two doors down just fine."

Connor hooked his finger under her chin and lifted her gaze to meet his. "Katie, I can tell somethin' is the matter. Was it because I kissed ye? Truly, I'd thought ye—"

"Why did you stop writing to me?" Kaitlyn blinked at the tears that pooled in her eyes. "I'm not accusing you or anything, Connor. I just want to understand. What happened? Was there someone else? Is that why you…" She couldn't finish the sentence and felt like an idiot. Here she was, just over twenty-four hours later, doing exactly what she'd told him she wouldn't do again—crying all over the place about their past relationship. But in her defense, quite a lot had changed since the pub.

For a few moments, Connor held her gaze, his expression tight. "Ye're right. I owe ye an explanation. 'Tis somethin' I should have given a long time ago." He led her to the soft chairs next to the fireplace, sitting her in one and bringing the other closer, facing her, so they sat nearly knee to knee.

Kaitlyn gripped her fingers tightly. What would he say? Would he tell her about falling in love with a beautiful woman he'd met at college? Or tell her how little by little, his feelings faded? She didn't know if she could stand hearing that truth. Sitting back into the depths of the plush chair, she twisted her fingers together. "You can tell me later. There's the treasure to worry about, and the terrorists. You have a lot more important things to deal with right now."

"Yer heart, it's always been important to me. I just took too long to realize it." He reached for her hands, resting his elbows on his knees as he spoke. "Katie, when ye'd left eight years ago, I can't describe how it hurt. I ached for ye, and every day I dreamed of the time we'd be together again. I threw myself into my studies, finishin' at the University as quickly as I could, and 'tis thrilled I was to be accepted into the Academy." Connor stopped talking. He rubbed his thumbs on the backs of Kaitlyn's hands.

She saw his eyes tense and dreaded what was to come.

"'Twas when I was still a cadet, I was assigned my first mission. I'm sure Seamus had somethin' to do with the post. New recruits didn't get chosen for operations like this. But 'twould give me experience, even though 'twas only a reconnaissance mission. Nothin' dangerous. We set up surveillance across the street from a suspected terrorist cell, and we'd record who went in and who went out. Took a few pictures. My handler, Daniel, worked under Seamus. He was a few years older than I. Probably about my age now. We talked a bit, and I told him about ye, and he told me about his new wife. They were expectin' a baby later that year." He blew out a breath.

"'Twas only a few more hours we had until our shift was over. Daniel, he sent me down the street to fetch some coffee. While I was gone, somehow the group we were watchin' must have been tipped off. I heard shots, but by the time I got back to the car, Daniel was dead. A drive-by shooting."

Kaitlyn felt a mixture of relief that Connor had escaped danger and sadness for his loss. She squeezed his hands. "Oh, Connor. That's terrible. I'm so sorry."

Connor nodded, and his shoulders sagged. "An hour later, I stood with Seamus on the porch of Daniel's house as he told a young wife that she was now a widow, and her husband, he wasn't comin' home again. I watched her break down, sobbing as Seamus did his best to comfort her, and all I could think of was ye, Katie. I never wanted ye to experience that knock on yer door."

"So, you just never talked to me again?" She spoke quietly, looking down at her hands.

"I tried a hundred times to write a letter or think of the words to say, but nothin' was right. So I acted the coward, and I'm sorry for it." Connor threaded his fingers through hers. "Then I learned ye were to be married. I knew I'd waited too long. I hated the idea of ye with another man." Still holding onto her hand, he lifted her chin. "Did ye love him, then?"

Kaitlyn studied his face. The face she knew so well. Small wrinkles formed around his eyes, as if he'd clenched his muscles, bracing himself for her answer. "Yes. No. Well, that is I didn't love him enough. Not as much as I should have." She shook her head. "I really wanted to. Todd was there the whole time my mom was sick. All through her chemo, her funeral, everything, and I couldn't let him go, because doing so felt like severing another link with my mom. How could I be with someone who never knew her? With her gone, I was alone, and the reality terrified me. I just figured the feelings would come in time. If I waited long enough, I'd love him. But it never happened, and pretending wasn't fair to either of us." Kaitlyn concentrated on their intertwined fingers. "And you never...I mean, didn't you...did you never have anyone else?"

"No one I'd consider marryin', though for a time I tried mighty hard to replace ye. But I've not stopped thinkin' of ye." He leaned closer. "And through these many years, I've not stopped lovin' ye."

At his words, her breath caught, and tears filled her eyes. He pulled her into his lap, and she buried her face in his neck as he held her.

"Don't cry, Katie. Please?" he murmured, lifting her face and brushing away her tears. "I've got ye back, and we've another chance now. Will ye forgive me then?"

Kaitlyn nodded. She pressed her hands on the sides of his face and swallowed before she finally regained control of her feelings. "All this time, I thought you'd found someone else, or you didn't want me."

"I never stopped wantin' ye, Katie," he whispered against her lips, sealing his mouth over hers.

Kaitlyn let herself get lost in the kiss, but doubts still tickled her thoughts. Could his explanation really be so simple? Could she trust him with her heart?

Chapter 25

Connor relished the feel of Katie in his arms—the taste of her lips and the softness of her skin. He'd kept his feelings buried for so long that their intensity took him by surprise. Telling Katie he was still in love with her terrified him. Exposing his true feelings made him vulnerable. But her acceptance brought relief. He'd finally found what he needed. Being with Katie, holding her soft body against his, was where he belonged and what he wanted. This feeling was what he'd been missing.

He skimmed his lips over her jaw, and she shivered in response as he kissed the soft skin beneath her ear lobe. Trailing kisses down her neck, he felt her pulse speed. He was desperate to make up for lost time and to erase the long years they'd been apart, but a small segment of his brain stopped him.

Instead, he cupped her face in his hands. "Katie."

She blinked open her eyes.

Looking into their depths, he nearly lost his reason. He shook his head to clear it. "Ye'll need to go to yer room now."

Her skin was hot and flushed. She raised her eyebrows in a silent question.

"If ye stay longer, I won't have the strength to let ye go." He saw a flash of something in her eyes that might have been disappointment, though the impression could have just been a suggestion of his ego.

She slid off his lap, wobbling on her injured feet.

He stood, holding onto her arm to steady her. Though his body cursed him, his brain told him he needed to give Katie time to process the things he'd said before going too far down this road. Especially after all the emotional ups and downs she'd been through the past few days. They both rode on the high of solving the riddle and of reuniting. She was vulnerable now, and he'd not have her doubting what they'd shared. "I want to do this right with ye, Katie. Not rush ye into anythin' ye'll regret. I'll not lose ye again."

Katie studied him for a moment. She raised one eyebrow, and her lips curled. "Could you at least kiss me again? I've waited such a long time."

Connor heard a hint of a tease in her voice. He smiled, brushing his lips softly across hers, and fought the impulse to deepen the kiss. He pulled her into an embrace and then walked down the hall to her room. Waiting until she unlocked her door, he pulled her into his arms again and trailed feather-light kisses across her neck, smiling when she sighed. "Sweet dreams, my Katie girl. And if ye've no plans for tomorrow mornin', I'd love yer company on a treasure hunt."

"Arrrgh." She grinned.

Connor pulled the door closed and listened to her turn the lock. Rather than return to his room, he leaned against the wall and waited for the sounds of her moving around her room as she prepared for bed to stop. For the first time since he'd returned to his apartment and found Seamus's letter, he felt at peace. Even though he still hadn't found the treasure, the search would take him, and by extension their enemies, away from the Manor House—and keep them away from the people he loved. He walked down the stairs and into the kitchen, finding leftovers in the refrigerator to reheat. As he ate, he firmed his plan in his mind.

The false coordinates he wrote would lead Robbie Lynch and his group to another area in the forest, a few miles from the location Seamus recorded. The area Connor chose was perfect for an ambush, heavily wooded on two sides with a lake on another. He'd wait until morning and call Jack with the location and the information to lay a trap. Then he'd give the coordinates to his enemies, and hopefully, all his problems would be solved—though in his experience things rarely turned out according to plan.

He didn't entertain the delusion every member of the R-IRA would immediately head to the location, but he was hopeful the ones who did would face enough retribution they'd abandon the hunt for Angus O'Brien's treasure.

Setting his dishes in the sink, he glanced at the clock. Only a few hours remained before he'd meet Katie for breakfast. The tension and adrenaline that kept him alert for so long were wearing off, and he was looking forward to some well-deserved sleep, even if he'd only manage a few hours. Letting himself into his room, he flipped on the light and bent to take off his shoes. Then something hard hit his head and the world went black.

Chapter 26

Connor eased open his eyes. His head swam, and the back of his skull throbbed. He reached up and tenderly touched the lump. His hair was sticky with blood. *What happened?* His mind groped as he tried to remember what was going on. He turned his head, blinking at the light. *Why am I on the floor?* Something floated at the edge of his mind...something important. Why couldn't he grab a hold of it?

"Took yer time about wakin' up, didn't ye?"

Connor shot upright—although the rush of nausea made him wish he'd moved a bit more slowly. He instinctively reached for his gun, his fingers sweeping over an empty holster and looked toward the speaker. The sluggishness in Connor's head was gone in an instant. His muscles clenched, and his gaze darted around his room, analyzing the situation and calculating his chances.

Robbie Lynch sat in a chair by the fire, a tumbler full of brandy in one hand and Connor's weapon in the other. He leaned back lazily, resting an ankle on his other knee. "And I don't think ye'll be wantin' to test my aim by making a run for it. Not when I might accidentally hit that fine bit o' skirt sleepin' down the hall. Or the old lady."

Connor's jaw clenched. He took a deep breath, beating back the hot fury that rose inside him. He knew

Lynch goaded to make him angry and pushed to make him careless. From his academy training, he knew emotions were his enemy in this situation. He forced his mind to be logical and think, but the pain in his head made reasoning difficult. *Concentrate.* He needed to get Lynch out of the manor house. Now. Before anyone woke up and found him here. Who knew what the thug would do? He glanced at the clock. He'd been unconscious longer than he'd thought. A cold sweat broke out on his skin when he realized Katie and Tillie would be awake within the hour.

"Have a seat then. I'll not envy ye the headache ye must have." Robbie pushed the other chair toward Connor with his foot.

Connor sat facing Lynch. He leaned back, mirroring Robbie's relaxed posture, though his mind raced.

Lynch set down his glass and turned the weapon over in his hands, checking the magazine before loading it back into the pistol with the heel of his hand, his movements showing proficiency with the weapon. He pulled back the slide and released the safety. "I knew somethin' about ye didn't ring true. My gaffer didna believe me. Thought we could trust ye, he did. But I knew. And now, will ye look at this weapon? A military issue SIG P226. I've seen one other—though this one is a newer model." He rubbed his chin. "'Twas quite recently actually. Nearby, just outside here. Near the pond. Ye must know the spot. 'Tis furious my gaffer was about how I handled Seamus O'Brien. He'll probably not appreciate how I'm plannin' on dealin' with yerself, either, Connor Flynn."

Connor's gut clenched as Lynch spoke of Seamus.

He crossed his arms and smiled, looking relaxed, though inside he was livid. "Aye, 'tis a nice gun. I'm quite fond of it."

"And here, the serial number tells me this gun is a government weapon. Now, why would ye be havin' somethin' like this, I'm askin' myself."

"They're not as rare as one might think. Pieces like this one sell for a nice price at the pawnshops in Dublin from time to time." Connor estimated how quickly he could move. Could he get the gun away from Lynch? He didn't think so. Not when Robbie Lynch possessed such an expert knowledge of the weapon. The man knew how to use it. Connor wasn't sure just how accurate his movements would be. He still fought his dizziness, and every movement accentuated the ache in his head.

Robbie continued studying the gun, waving it toward Connor as he spoke. "From the first moment I saw ye in Lyon's Pub, I could tell ye were in law enforcement. Let me guess, G-2?"

"'Tis interesting, that. I'd no impression that ye were anythin' but a hired thug from the first moment I saw *ye*. Are ye tellin' me what yer doin' in my room in the middle of the night? Accordin' to yer gaffer, I've until noon to hand over the treasure. Truthfully, 'tis been a long day and—"

Faster than Connor would have thought possible, Lynch sprang out of his chair and struck him across the face. Connor nearly lost consciousness again as his head hit the back of the chair. Warm blood trickled beneath his eye, but he refused to give Lynch the satisfaction of seeing him touch his face. Connor curled his lip, looking at Lynch mockingly. "I was right. Had ye any real training, ye'd have learned how to hit."

Lynch's nostrils flared. He waved the gun beneath Connor's nose. "I've had enough of yer cheek. Ye'll be givin' me the treasure and the charms now, and we're through discussin' it."

"Well, as I was tellin' ye earlier, I'll need the time we'd agreed upon to get the treasure." Lynch struck him again.

This time, Connor's eyes filled, and he heard a crunch in his nose. *Bollocks*. Through the pain, he managed a smirk. Lynch leaned close enough that Connor smelled the liquor on his breath and saw the sweat on his brow.

"Ye've discovered the treasure sure enough. I received a report tellin' me ye'd found it with yer *oul doll* not two hours ago." He glanced toward the door. "I'm wastin' my time talkin' to ye when 'twould be so much more pleasurable to get the information from her." He turned toward the door.

At the insinuation, a surge of fear shot through Connor, and he struggled to keep his voice steady. Someone at the Manor House had been watching them. He brushed imaginary lint flecks off his sleeve and straightened the pleats in his pants. "'Tis true, we found the hidin' place, but the treasure 'twasn't there. It's been moved. Most likely by Seamus, though he left the coordinates." He touched his jacket pocket then jerked away his hand as if the action had been a mistake.

Lynch snatched the paper from his pocket, smirking as he studied it. "There now. That wasn't too hard, was it? I'll even take care of the final step, though I'll be askin' ye to come along for the ride. Don't be worryin' yerself. We'll not be lonely. Plenty of friends will meet us there."

Thoughts spun through Connor's mind. He needed to call Jack. The group would only search for the treasure for so long before they realized they'd been tricked, and they'd return for Katie. He needed the reinforcements. But Robbie Lynch wouldn't let him out of his sight, and Connor couldn't contact his boss without his phone.

Right now, his primary objective was to get Lynch far away from the manor house and protect Katie and Tillie. The secondary objective was apprehension of the men who threatened them, although if he failed in that endeavor, Katie and Tillie would still be in danger. Most likely, he wouldn't survive to protect them. If only he could get a message to Katie. If only his head wasn't so murky. He'd need all his wits if he was to outsmart Lynch.

"Shall we, then?" Lynch said, sweeping one hand toward the door. The other held Connor's gun.

Connor didn't move. "When she finds I've gone, she'll call up the *guarda*. She has the coordinates, and she'll follow. I'll need to leave her a note." He took a deep breath and let it out slowly. "She'll need to believe I've left her." 'Twasn't too difficult to pretend his heart was hurtin'. He didn't entertain much hope of seein' Katie again. Once his usefulness was spent, he didn't imagine Lynch and his group would leave him alive.

Lynch studied Connor for a moment before his face relaxed, and a cruel sneer curled his lip. "'Tis perfect, that. I think I'd prefer ye accompanyin' me with no hope of rescue. And yer poor broken heart 'twill be the icing on the cake."

Connor made a show of leaning forward, rubbing

the back of his head as he slipped his phone out of his pocket with his other hand, and pressed it between the cushions of the chair. He stood and walked to the desk. He felt Lynch's gaze as he pulled out a piece of paper and scrawled a short note. Folding it, he wrote *Kaitlyn* on the outside, hoping she'd understand what he was telling her.

Lynch snatched the note out of his hand, unfolded it, read it, and then nodded. "And so tragic 'tis to see true love's hopes dashed." He smirked and handed it back to Connor. "Shall we slide it under her door, then?"

Connor shook his head. No way in hell would he let Robbie Lynch anywhere near Katie's room. He propped the note against the pillows on his bed, praying Katie would understand what he needed her to do and praying she'd be safe. If someone had indeed told Robbie Lynch they'd found the treasure, chances were, *that* someone still watched her.

"We'll be takin' yer car if ye don't mind." Lynch held up Connor's keys.

Connor glanced back one more time at the folded paper that held his hopes for all their safety and then followed his enemy from the room.

Chapter 27

Kaitlyn,

Truly, I'm sorry for not having the courage to tell you in person, but when you find this letter, I'll be gone. I said yesterday as we walked half way south on the road toward Máire, and again as you sat on the stairs that I cared for you. However, upon further reflection, those words were expressed in the heat of the moment and shouldn't have been uttered. It seems I've become too much like my gaffer and have no time for a relationship. Remember, the words the Holy Father told you were true. I apologize for not saying good-bye, but I'd ask you not to call or come after me or the treasure. I'll not be back.

Connor

Kaitlyn sat on the edge of Connor's bed, staring at nothing. The note hung from her loose hand. At seven o'clock sharp, she'd waited on a chair in the main hall with her purse, jacket, and a backpack loaded with sandwiches and water bottles. She'd been unable to force her swollen feet into shoes and resigned herself to wearing her rubber-soled slippers for a few days. When Connor still hadn't come down ten minutes later, she'd worried he'd slept in. Though he undoubtedly needed the rest, she was sure the "meet the terrorists with the coordinates of the secret treasure" appointment was one he wouldn't want to be late for. Finally, climbing painfully back up the stairs, she knocked on his door, only to find it ajar. Connor was gone.

Kaitlyn deflated. She stood and limped toward the bedroom door. What had she done wrong? Something must have changed in the few hours since he'd kissed her good night which made him unable to even stand the idea of seeing her one more time. She was numb, feeling too empty even for tears. She must have scared him away, been too needy, or too obvious in how she felt. Weren't girls supposed to play a little hard to get?

And his note. The wording was strange. The phrasing didn't even sound like him. Had he been drinking? A glass holding an amber drink sat on the side table next to his chair. She changed direction and walking to the small table, picked up the tumbler, and sniffed. Strong liquor. The alcohol could be the reason for the crazy rambling in the letter. Drinking himself into incoherency a few hours before they were to meet the enemy didn't make sense. Wouldn't he have wanted his mind alert? Sickness replaced the hollow feeling. Not to mention the flash of anger that heated her cheeks. Had he tricked her and taken the treasure? Had he been in league with the terrorists all along? Had he lied to her and to Aunt Tillie?

Again, she glanced at the note. Did Connor always use such proper speech when he wrote and spelling out words like "you"? She didn't know. And *Kaitlyn*. He'd never called her that. She couldn't even imagine how his voice would sound saying her full name. Only once, she remembered when he'd introduced her to the waitress in the pub. Brianna. He'd called her Kaitlyn then, but when they were alone, he'd always called her Katie. By deliberately avoiding his pet name for her, he gave the appearance of distancing himself.

Was he expecting someone else to read the message? The idea was so humiliating Kaitlyn tore the letter into small squares. What if she hadn't been the one to find the letter? It hadn't been sealed. Her stomach clenched at the very idea Aunt Tillie or one of the staff could have found it and seen how gullible she was. Was Connor rubbing the fact in her face that he didn't care if someone else read it before her?

She sprinkled a few little squares over the cold logs in Connor's fireplace when she jolted. Connor *didn't* care if someone else read it before her! What if someone else had been with him, and Connor deliberately left an odd-sounding letter only she would understand? *No! No! No!* Kaitlyn dropped to her knees and frantically picked the scraps of paper out of the ashes. *This desperation is ridiculous.* She was just clinging to a last pathetic hope for Connor—like she always had. *Am I really digging through charred wood to put together a puzzle and decode a secret message?* The whole idea was insane but not more insane than terrorists searching for a treasure hidden in a statue's leg.

When she was sure she'd retrieved all the scraps, she spread the bits of paper on the wood floor and leaned back against one of the leather chairs. Charcoal covered her fingertips, and she was careful to touch only the edges of the pieces as she slid them around, reconstructing the message. Her fingers shook and reacted clumsily as she hurried. If he'd really left her an encoded message, and he was in trouble, she'd just made it worse by wasting all this time feeling sorry for herself.

Once all the scraps were back together, Kaitlyn looked over the dirty, uneven mess that moments earlier had been a clean piece of paper with Connor's tidy block letter writing. She read the lines, searching for something, anything that might make sense, but the note just seemed to be gibberish.

She didn't remember sitting on the stairs, at all. Was she supposed to find something there? She'd already walked on the stairs twice today, and dozens of other feet would be tromping up and down them. He wouldn't leave something for her that anyone could find. And they'd been on the road only briefly before they got to his car, but she hadn't walked, he'd carried her. And he hadn't told her he cared about her then. Not until they sat here in his room, he—Kaitlyn used the chair arm to stand as the questions spun through her mind. She sat in one of the chairs. What did Connor want her to do?

She chewed on her nails, feeling frustrated. Looking at the clock, she realized nearly an hour had passed since Connor was supposed to have met her. Over four hours since he'd left her at her door, and who knew what had happened since? What kind of trouble was he in? Was he hurt? Or worse? She smacked her hands against the arms of the chair and looked back at the note. *This spot* was where he'd talked to her last night. Was something special about the chair? She pressed her fingers into the gap around the edge of the seat cushion and brushed against something. Her heart beat harder as she pulled Connor's phone out of the gap. A warm swell of pride grew in her chest. She could almost hear his voice in her head telling her he knew she could do it.

Come on, Connor. Who do you want me to call? She looked back at the note, and the answer jumped out. Connor's gaffer. His boss. What was his name again? Jack. Kaitlyn scrolled through the contact list until she found it. No last name, no other information— just a phone number.

Kaitlyn's heart raced as Connor's plan dawned on her. She pushed Call and pulled the folded paper with Seamus's coordinates out of her purse that rested against her hip.

"Flynn." A low gravelly voice answered on the first ring.

"No. Jack...um...Hi. My name's Kaitlyn Donovan. I'm Connor's friend, and he's in trouble. Can you record this call, or write down the information or something? I'll read off some numbers." Kaitlyn read the numbers from Seamus's note slowly and clearly. "Did you get those?"

"Aye. From the looks of them, 'tis GPS coordinates ye've told me. Now, lass, I'll be needin' to know the whole story. Where's Flynn? What's the trouble he's in? And how did ye come by his phone, then?"

Kaitlyn stood and walked toward the door. "I don't know everything. But Connor's been taken. I think that's where he is, and he needs help."

As she reached the door and pulled it open, she watched Ian step through into Connor's room. Of course, she'd forgotten to cancel her tennis lesson. She put up one finger, telling Ian to wait.

"Listen, I'm leaving now, and I'll meet—"

Ian took the phone.

She whipped around her head. "Ian, that was a

214

really important—" But her words caught in her throat as she saw Ian no longer wore his cheerful expression but a calculating frown, which made him look nearly unrecognizable. Cold tingles of dread washed over her.

He dropped the phone into the half-full tumbler of liquor and seized her arm. "I was beginnin' to worry ye'd not come down for yer lesson this mornin'. We've unfinished business with yer fella, and 'twouldn't have the same effect without ye there."

Without his cheerful smile, Ian's eyes looked cold. A heavy dread settled in her chest. His hold on her arm was painful. "Ian, what are you doing?" Kaitlyn jerked, pulling from his grip.

His fingers tightened. He turned her toward him, opening his jacket to show a gun tucked into the waistband of his warm-up pants. "Now, from what I hear, ye gave my friends a bit o' trouble last time ye were asked to come along calmly. I'll not mince words this time, so we'll have no danger of miscommunication. If ye can't walk down the steps nicely and get into my car, I'll be putting a bullet into that old lady downstairs. Do ye understand, Kaitlyn?"

Kaitlyn nodded, feeling numb. She was too shocked to say anything as she allowed herself to be led out of Connor's room and down the hall.

Ian slid his hand down her arm to hold hers.

She repressed a shudder at his touch as they descended the stairs.

Different scenarios played out in her mind, but none made what was happening any more real. Ian. Gentle, happy Ian had just threatened to murder her sweet aunt. As terror constricted her lungs, Kaitlyn struggled to breathe. Would Aunt Tillie hear them?

Would she be in the Great Hall? What would Ian do if Aunt Tillie stopped them before they left the Manor House?

The sounds of voices and the clank of dishes floated out of the dining room as they walked past.

"Ian, where's Connor?" She wished she could keep her voice from shaking.

"We'll join him soon enough, then."

Thankfully, they walked through the Great Hall and out the main doors without running into anyone. Kaitlyn darted her eyes around, looking for the guards. She had no idea if they would even see her. Besides, she'd been with Ian so often during the past few weeks, the guards likely wouldn't think anything of seeing them together.

Ian's grip tightened.

She stifled the urge to scream for help. She couldn't risk the chance he would follow through on his promise and hurt Aunt Tillie.

"Don't ye even be thinkin' about tryin' anything, Kaitlyn," Ian said. "And don't fool yerself to think I'd hesitate killin' ye or yer aunt."

The menace in his voice chilled her. He kept a grip on her hand as he opened the passenger door, and her last bit of hope flew away when the man with the gold tooth stepped out.

"Lovely to see ye again, Miss Donovan," Gold Tooth said with a small bow.

"Ye'll need to be ridin' in the back, Kenneth," Ian said. "'Twill appear a bit more convincin' to the security as a group of mates on a day trip with Kaitlyn wavin' merrily from the front seat."

Kenneth muttered a few choice words as he leaned

the seat forward and climbed into the hatch-back's small rear bench.

"Get in." Ian clicked the seat into place and pushed Kaitlyn into the car then walked around and slid behind the steering wheel. He pulled the car onto the long drive.

"Why are you doing this?" Kaitlyn didn't care that her voice trembled.

Ian glanced at her before looking back at the road. "Time to smile for the guards." He pulled the gun from his waist band and held it on his lap with his right hand, aiming the barrel across his legs toward Kaitlyn. As they passed through the gates, he lifted the fingers of the hand on the steering wheel in a friendly wave.

Kaitlyn was amazed at the transformation in his face as he grinned to the guards. She waved, too, hoping they couldn't see her hand shaking.

The guard signaled them through without even stopping the car.

Ian turned onto the main road, driving away from Tullybrae.

"Why are you working with these people, Ian?" Kaitlyn asked. Of course he'd been misled. If she could only convince him. "Don't you know who they are? What they've done?"

Ian darted a look at her. "And who are they, Kaitlyn?"

"Terrorists. They're with the R-IRA." She pointed toward Kenneth in the back seat, who smiled with his shiny gold tooth and wiggled his fingers in a sarcastic wave.

Ian's face broke into a grin. "Are they now?"

The smile wasn't the one she'd grown used to

seeing. "I don't know what they've told you, or how they convinced you to...do this, but it's not too late, Ian." She touched his arm. "We can fix this. You don't have to let them manipulate you into doing something you'll regret."

His gaze snapped to her face. "What makes ye think I've been talked into anything?"

"Because you're not like these guys."

"Aye, and it's true enough." Kenneth spoke up from the back seat. "He's not like the rest of us, because he's our gaffer, is Ian."

Kaitlyn twisted in her seat, looking at Kenneth's face, hoping she'd see evidence he was joking, but her stomach turned over when she saw his expression was serious. "No, Ian, it's not true. You can't be... Why would you?"

Ian's mouth was stretched into a thin line.

Any trace of the happy, joking tennis player had disappeared, only to be replaced by a man who looked years older and hardened. "Ye've no idea what 'tis like to have invaders in yer land, Kaitlyn. To have yer government led by those who've no love for Ireland or her people. We're Revolutionaries, not fanatics, fightin' against enemies who insist on occupyin' our country. *They're* the terrorists," he said with an ugly twist to his mouth. "They've left us no other recourse but violence. 'Tisn't how the media would have ye believe, Kaitlyn. We're not randomly killin' innocent people."

Ian spoke softly. His eyes shone with conviction. As Kaitlyn listened, she almost felt sorry for him. Almost. "Uncle Seamus wasn't hurting your cause."

"'Twas unfortunate, that. Seamus'ss death wasn't a decision I approved. Some of our members aren't as adept at following orders."

"Lynch wouldn't have had to kill him if he'd just handed over the bloody trinkets," Kenneth muttered.

"He's been nothin' but trouble this entire operation, Lynch," Ian said, glaring at Kenneth in the rearview mirror. "Killin' Seamus was just the start. All that investigatin' as a result could have blown my cover. Not to mention his mistake, approachin' the priest and puttin' Tillie on her guard. Then takin' Kaitlyn—I told ye I'd get the pendant *my* way."

"We were getting' tired of waitin' for ye to romance it away from her."

Ian's gaze darted toward Kaitlyn.

She turned away, disgusted for letting Kenneth's words hurt her feelings. So, their plan was the reason he'd been so friendly to her. So much for him being smitten by her smiling eyes. *Wow. Just when I thought my dating track record couldn't get any worse.*

Kaitlyn looked out the window as the men argued. The car had been twisting and turning over the country roads. Now, she could see they approached the more densely populated roads of a city. Ennis, she assumed. She could only hope and pray Jack was on his way to rescue them.

Kenneth's cell phone rang, and he answered, speaking for a moment, then handed it between the seats to Ian. "'Tis Lynch," he said. "He and Flynn just now arrived at the site."

At the sound of Connor's name, Kaitlyn jerked, her heart flying into her throat. She listened to Ian and strained her ears to hear the other side of the conversation. Apparently, Lynch rounded up a group to search the GPS location with shovels and metal detectors. Connor was with them.

As they talked, Kaitlyn swallowed against a dry mouth. They were at the site, and they were searching for the treasure, Connor was their prisoner, and she didn't hear a team of secret agents jumping out to apprehend them. Where was Jack? Hadn't he understood the message? She'd given him the coordinates. What was she missing?

She went over Connor's note again in her mind, looking out the window at the city of Ennis. The streets were narrow and curving, lined with colorful buildings. They passed a beautiful blue river running through the city and a church. Something hovered just outside of Kaitlyn's consciousness, but she couldn't quite seize the detail.

She tried again, concentrating. A church. *Máire*. Connor mentioned Máire in his letter. Well, he'd mentioned the road, though not calling it by its name was strange. What were his exact words? Something about halfway south down the road, so halfway down Four-Mile Road was two miles. *What* was two miles?

A rush of adrenaline spiked through her veins, and she jolted, glancing toward Ian to see if he'd noticed.

But he still talked on the phone, weaving his way through the winding streets.

Two miles! Of course, Connor didn't give Robbie Lynch the correct coordinates. He'd never have told them Seamus's secret. He'd sent the terrorists two miles south. That meant she'd given Jack the wrong location—the location of the treasure, but the coordinates wouldn't take him to Connor or the terrorists. She'd ruined any hope Connor had of rescue.

Kaitlyn's mind spun. Who knew how long they had

until Robbie Lynch and his group figured out they were searching in the wrong area? What would he do to Connor? Surely not bid him good day and return him to the manor. *Kaitlyn,* not Jack, was Connor's only hope of rescue. Anyway, what did she have to lose? Without a doubt, the terrorists would kill both of them once they had the treasure. The chance of getting away from Ian and Kenneth was so slim…but, at least 'twas a chance.

Ian pulled onto another narrow road bordered by rows of buildings. The traffic grew heavier as they rounded a curve and drove past a crowded town square. The city appeared to be having a fair, or perhaps a farmers' market. Kaitlyn knew she had a chance. Stealing one last look toward Ian, she said a quick prayer and held tight to her purse. Then pushing open the door, she leaped from the car.

Although Ian hadn't been driving fast, Kaitlyn still hit the pavement harder than she'd expected, slamming her forehead against the curb. White lights appeared in front of her eyes, and the world started slipping away. *No!* She fought to maintain her consciousness and, at the same time, scrambled as fast as she could away from the road and into the crowd.

She knew Ian couldn't stop the car in the middle of the street, and Kenneth would have to climb over the seat to get out. Those precious seconds would make all the difference, and she couldn't waste them. She turned her head from side to side, searching for a path as she pushed through the crowd, not sure which way to run. She felt curious glances and resisted the urge to turn around. Something stung her eye, and she realized her head was bleeding. No wonder people stared. Between her dizziness and her throbbing feet, she knew she couldn't run very long. She needed somewhere to hide and contact Jack.

Kaitlyn ducked behind an ice cream stand, pressing her hand against the booth as she fought her wooziness. She touched her head and pulled away fingers covered with blood. Nausea churned in her stomach. She really needed to sit down.

"And what are ye doin' back here?"

She heard the voice and turned, blinking to bring the person into focus. A boy with a sticky face peered at her. She guessed he was about twelve. "Lookin' for free ice cream, are ye?" His eyes widened when he looked at her head. "Ye'll be needin' help then, miss." He dug around in the ice cream booth's supplies and handed her a wad of napkins.

"I need a cab," she said, frustrated at her slurred words.

"As ye like." He took her hand to guide her from behind the booth.

Kaitlyn dug in her heels. She was having a hard time concentrating. "I can't go out there. Ian... He'll find me."

The boy pulled her back into the shadows. "'Tis the *guarda* I should be callin'. They'll sort yer Ian out."

Kaitlyn shook her head then wished she hadn't. "Please, I just need a cab." Why couldn't she think straight?

The boy nodded, pulled her behind the booth, and through the shadowy maze of boxes and temporary wooden structures.

She stumbled, tripping over extension cords and equipment. The edges of her vision were turning gray. They reached the end of a row, and he told her to wait, disappearing into the sunlight. Kaitlyn held the napkins to her head. She leaned against the back of a booth, shifting her weight against the sharp pains in her feet, wondering if the boy would return. Should she just leave? But the thought of walking into the open where Ian could find her caused cold fear to slice through her. She fought against the darkness at the edge of her vision, knowing as long as she stood on her throbbing feet, she wouldn't fall asleep. After what seemed like forever, but was probably only a few minutes, she felt a tug on her hand.

"I've a cab waitin', miss."

Kaitlyn stumbled behind him as he led her along the edge of the town square and across the street to a waiting cab.

The cab driver held the door.

Gratefully, she slid onto the seat, reaching into her purse to grab a few bills which she pressed into the boy's hand and blinked again as she focused on the grin that lit up his face.

He saluted her and ran back into the crowd.

"I need you to take me north," she said to the cab driver. "To a druid's circle about ten miles north of town. Do you know where it is?"

"Miss, I'll not be tellin' ye yer business, but what ye need is a doctor. Leave the magic for another day."

"Please." Kaitlyn swayed.

"Sure, and yer the payin' customer, though I'm of a mind that a hospital is where ye'll find true healin'."

Kaitlyn felt the car move, and she knew she was safe for now.

The drive took nearly a half hour, and Kaitlyn spent the entire trip struggling to force her heavy eyelids to stay open. She probably had a concussion and knew if she slept, she might not wake up to tell Jack where to find Connor. She also fought against the nausea churning in her stomach, and the hills and curves of the country road weren't helping.

Finally, the cab driver stopped the car and helped her out. "'Tis just off the road here a bit." He led her through the forest. "I'll not leave ye here alone. Ye'll be needin' to see a doctor as soon as ye find out that yer ancient mysticism won't actually cure anything."

The shooting pains that jabbed through Kaitlyn's feet at each step were what kept her conscious, and she stumbled along until they stepped into the clearing. She pressed her hand against a stone to keep herself from collapsing. "Jack!" she called, though she could tell her voice didn't carry far. "Jack, it's me, Kaitlyn." Tears filled her eyes, the sound of her yelling causing her head to pound. "Jack." Her voice was even softer now. She just didn't have the strength to yell again.

The darkness she'd fought so long closed in. Kaitlyn was almost ready to succumb to it when a group of soldiers stormed out of the forest. She turned to see a terrified cab driver on his knees with his hands raised and a dozen rifles pointed at him.

A broad-shouldered man with a salt-and-pepper crew cut stepped forward and caught her as she fell, easing her to the ground.

He turned and yelled over his shoulder for someone to bring smelling salts then turned back. "Well, Kaitlyn. A pleasure 'tis to meet ye in person. Jack Murphy."

Chapter 28

Connor watched the group scour the clearing. He shifted his position and winced, certain he had at least a few cracked ribs. One of his eyes was swollen shut, and a drop of blood slid down his cheek and onto his already spotted shirt. He closed his eyes, clearing his head to assess the situation.

They'd arrived at the site nearly two hours after Lynch had taken him from the manor. The time between had been spent driving around County Clare while Lynch made phone call after phone call, gathering men to help with the search for the treasure. Once they'd arrived at the coordinates, Lynch kept his weapon trained on Connor as he leaned against the car, certainly scratching the paint. The two had watched while the group systematically wove back and forth across the area with their metal detectors.

Lynch answered his phone.

Connor listened to his side of the conversation with Ian. He realized Katie attempted an escape, and her captors were in pursuit. The idea of her feeling terrified, being chased through unfamiliar streets on her raw feet, was enough to spur him into action. While Lynch was still distracted by the phone call, Connor kicked the thug's feet out from under him and slammed his shoulder into the bullet wound on Lynch's arm.

Escaping and finding Katie dominated his

thoughts. But his bound hands and the fact he was vastly outnumbered cut his doomed effort short. When he'd regained consciousness for the second time in the space of a few hours, he found himself sitting on the mossy ground a few yards away, his arms stretched around a tree and tied behind him.

Shoulders aching, he strained against the restraints, but the knots gave no slack. Frustrated, he turned his attention back to the group, studying them for weaknesses, and scanning the area for escape routes. But he'd chosen this particular location for that very reason—as a place to trap his enemies, and the chance of him getting loose and escaping from twenty men was slim. He prayed Katie was more successful.

As if in answer to his thoughts, Ian's absurd, blue hatch-back pulled into the clearing. He and another man climbed out and looked around for a second before storming toward Lynch.

Katie wasn't with them. Though Connor couldn't hear what they said, from their gestures and angry expressions, he assumed they hadn't recaptured her. He smiled. *Aye, that's my Katie-girl.* He even allowed a small bit of hope into his chest. Would she get a hold of Jack? Not if she hadn't understood the letter. She'd most likely go straight to the *guarda.* But if she hadn't figured out his clues in the first place, she wouldn't lead them to the right location.

As the small chance for rescue became even smaller, he slumped, his heart sinking a bit. But he held onto the hope that Katie would be safe—that she'd find a way to protect herself and Tillie. Maybe even take her back to the states. At this point, wishing for their safety was all he had. Ian and Lynch wouldn't keep him alive much longer. They became more frustrated with the search. Without Katie to be used as a hostage to force him to talk, keeping a prisoner, especially a dangerous one, was more of a liability than an asset.

Thoughts of Katie weighed down his chest. He imagined her soft curls, the dimples that dipped into her cheeks when she smiled. After all this time he'd found her, only to lose her again. So much had changed in the few days they'd been together. *He'd* changed. He'd seen a chance the two of them might have a life together. Though having her for a short time was bittersweet, he wouldn't have changed anything. He'd told her he loved her, and that he'd always loved her. He hoped the knowledge would be a comfort, and she could go on without him.

Lynch and Ian walked toward him.

Connor lifted his chin. "I expected a bit more of ye to be certain, Ian. Bein' outsmarted by a woman. And an American at that?" He baited him, hoping Ian would lose his temper and give more information on what happened with Katie.

Stepping closer, Ian kicked him in the side.

The man was too predictable. A flare of pain shot through him as his already cracked ribs took the impact. He gasped, praying he didn't have a punctured lung. Taking a shallow breath, he forced a sneer to his face. "No matter what ye tried, Katie couldna' get away from ye fast enough."

Ian shifted his weight to deliver another kick.

Connor was ready and lashed out with his leg, making contact with Ian's knee and causing it to buckle. The effort nearly pulled Connor's shoulders out of the socket, but he didn't allow the pain to show.

Ian fell awkwardly and rolled on the ground, holding his knee. He glared at Connor with cold eyes in his red face. "Kill him, Lynch."

Connor heard Lynch's gun cock next to his ear. He clenched his jaw and focused on the memory of Katie's brown eyes while he braced himself for the explosion.

The pop of a gunfire sounded.

Connor jerked. Then he realized the noise came from a distance. He looked across the clearing and saw Jack lowering his weapon. Conner barely registered Robbie Lynch crumpling to the ground next to him, the soldiers flooding the area, or the sounds of yelling and gunfire. All he saw was Katie across the clearing, and his tensed muscles sagged as waves of warm relief poured over him.

Katie screamed his name and struggled against Jack who held her arm, restraining her.

Soon, Jack decided the area was secure, and finally gave in, allowing her to stumble in her slippers across the clearing to Connor.

She reached him and fell to her knees in front of him.

Katie held his head between her hands, pressing kisses on the parts of his face he assumed weren't bleeding. One side of her face was caked in trails of blood from a gash on her forehead. Her eyes were red and swollen, and her nose dripped. She sobbed, making a wet choking, squeaking noise. Connor had never seen anything so beautiful in his life.

"Ye did it, Katie girl. I knew ye'd do it."

"Connor, I thought I'd never…that you were…and then when I saw…"

"I know, but 'tis all right now. And nothin' will

take ye away from me again."

Someone freed his hands, and he wrapped his arms around her, pushing his fingers into her hair and lifting her lips to meet his. The adrenaline that spiked through him moments before only increased as Katie's soft body melted against him, her touch causing his blood to heat. He moved his lips over hers, their kisses intensifying as he realized he believed he'd hold her again.

A shadow stretched across them as someone stepped in front of the sun.

"While 'tis the most lovely thing I've witnessed in a long time, to be sure." Jack's voice held a smile. "But I'm afraid I'll need to be gettin' the two of ye to a hospital. I've no doubt yer lass suffered a fairly serious concussion, though she'd not hear of allowin' anyone to treat it until we'd found ye. Aye, and from the looks of it, Connor, ye didn't fare much better with this lot. Quite a pair, the two of ye."

Katie sighed and rested her head against Connor's shoulder.

The pressure increased as she leaned more heavily against him for support. She didn't resist when a pair of medics lifted her.

Jack supported Connor as he stood, and the group made its way through the mess of injuries, arrests, and weapons confiscation that marred the formerly peaceful clearing.

Connor rubbed his shoulders and gingerly pressed his side, wincing.

"A keeper, that one." Jack motioned with his head toward Katie, who was being gently lowered into the back of Jack's car.

The medic laid her down on the seat.

Her eyes were closed, and her only movement was the gentle rise and fall of her breathing.

A swell of tenderness rose in his chest. "Aye, and I'm plannin' on it, Jack."

Chapter 29

Kaitlyn opened her eyes. She felt dizzy and woozy as her senses were dulled by medication. The sterile smell of a hospital hit her nose. She sat up blinking and looked around, but the action made her head pound so she again laid back. The room was dimly lit with a fluorescent bulb, and she had no idea what time it was, or even whether the time was day or night.

A figure rose from a chair in the darkened corner.

Fear jolted in her chest. But the danger had passed. She was safe now, wasn't she? "Connor?"

"No, my love, 'tis just myself." Tillie's familiar voice warmed her heart.

"Oh, Aunt Tillie." Relief filled her as Kaitlyn reached for her aunt's hand. "I'm so glad you're here. Is Connor okay?"

Tillie squeezed her hand. "Sure, and he's doin' fine. Left the hospital a few hours ago with Jack. Apparently, quite a bit of paperwork needs to be completed after yer adventure yesterday." Tillie helped Kaitlyn adjust the hospital bed.

"Yesterday…" Kaitlyn calculated how long she'd been asleep, but thinking made her brain hurt. She reached her fingers to touch the injury on her forehead, only to find it wrapped in bandages.

Tillie pulled down Kaitlyn's hand to her lap. "The doctors tell me it's lucky ye are that a minor concussion's all the damage done to yer head. Yer feet, though. They're another story altogether. It appears ye've been runnin' about County Clare with five broken toes. From what the doctor told me, each step ye took must have been excruciatin'."

Kaitlyn looked down at her feet. Even with the wrappings, they were every bit as sore as before. She tugged at the sheets, but even that bit of movement hurt her head.

Tillie gently lifted the bedding off her legs and showed her the wrappings on both feet.

Kaitlyn groaned, leaning back her head against the pillows.

A knock sounded at the door.

Tillie tucked the sheets around Kaitlyn's legs before she opened it.

The bright lights of the hall cast the two men in shadows as they entered the room, but she'd recognize his silhouette anywhere. Relief filled her. "Connor."

He stepped to the bed and took her hand, threading his fingers through hers and pressing a kiss to her lips.

The other man who entered flipped on the light. "So yer awake, then. We've a bit to discuss, if yer feelin' up to it."

"Jack, the lights," Tillie exclaimed. "Have a bit of courtesy. My niece has suffered a concussion. And keep yer voice low. 'Tis a hospital, for heaven's sake."

"No, Aunt Tillie, it's all right. You can leave on the lights." Now that she could see Connor, she examined his face. His cheek had a line of stitches, and a blotchy mess of bruises colored his jaw and one eye.

"Looks bad, doesn't it?" he asked.

"I like it. You look like Rocky Balboa," Kaitlyn

said, her lips curving into a smile. "Not as bad as having a bandage around your head and casts on your feet."

"Sure, and yer beautiful, Katie." His lips brushed hers again. He pulled away and gently traced his finger around her lips. His eyes held her gaze.

Jack cleared his throat. "If ye don't mind, I'll be remindin' ye that other people still exist on this planet besides yerselves, then. I've a few more loose ends to tie up in the investigation, and I'll leave the two of ye alone."

Connor turned to sit on the edge of the bed, the twisting causing him to wince and hold his side.

She scooted her feet out of the way so he wouldn't bump them.

"Agent Flynn's asked me not to debrief ye until ye've fully recovered," Jack said. "However, I'd like to give a bit of an update, if 'tis alright."

Seeing Kaitlyn's nod, Jack pointed at the two of them. "Just so ye know, yer actions yesterday resulted in the apprehension…or neutralization of seventeen members of the R-IRA. A few in particular were key players and leaders in their operation. We've invested a great deal of manpower and funding into discovering their whereabouts. One man, Ian he was callin' himself, we believe to be one of the highest rankin' leaders in their organization. We'd not seen a picture of him or known his name until now."

Jack shifted his weight, leaning closer to the bed. "Ye can be confident ye've saved lives by what ye did yesterday, Kaitlyn."

Connor squeezed her hand, winking with his good eye.

Kaitlyn's heart swelled. Jack's words and Connor's acknowledgement filled her with pride. But at the same time, she hated all this attention. She hadn't done it by herself. If not for Connor's letter...she shuddered, thinking of what could have happened.

"Ye should be proud of yerself, Kaitlyn Donovan." The skin around Jack's eyes crinkled in a smile.

"Thank you. But I didn't do it alone. Connor's the one—"

"Aye, and don't ye worry, we'll not forget to give Agent Flynn his due credit. As his superior officer, I'm expectin' a promotion myself, and I'll be puttin' in his name to replace me." Jack turned his gaze to Connor. "Other jobs are available at the agency, Flynn. Not all involve line-of-fire missions. Ye've the perfect mentality and qualities for a supervisor."

Connor squinted, his brow furrowing.

Kaitlyn could tell he was processing the things Jack said. Would he be happy as a supervisor? Would he want to give up the front-line undercover missions? "I guess I don't understand what the terrorists wanted with the treasure."

"Funding." Connor turned back toward her. "'Tis difficult to get a loan for somethin' like a dirty bomb or weapons cache." He lifted his top lip in a sneer. "Who'll be knowin' what plans they had for the money, but ye can rest assured, 'twouldn't be pretty."

"But a treasure never existed, did it?" Kaitlyn asked.

"Actually, that brings us to another item I've a need to discuss with the three of ye." Jack took a step back and spread his arm toward Tillie.

From where she'd been sitting quietly, Tillie

stepped up to the other side of the bed, taking Kaitlyn's fingers, carefully avoiding the IV needle in the back of her hand.

"I sent a group back to the druid ring this mornin' while ye were all sleepin' away in yer hospital beds. They located and returned with an ammunition box, which I took the liberty of openin', since it pertained to my investigation." Jack reached into his jacket pocket. "Inside, I found this." He handed a clear plastic bag to Tillie.

"What is this, then?" She reached inside with trembling hands and pulled out a folded piece of paper, spreading it on her knee.

The three others leaned closer to read the now-recognizable bold handwriting which had belonged to Seamus. The note was brief—just the name of a bank and a row of numbers.

"'Tis an account set up by Seamus," Jack said. "In all three of yer names. I took a peek at the amount. From the look of the total, he cashed out quite a grand treasure. Seems the old boy was lookin' out for his family from the get-go."

A tear dropped onto the paper, and Kaitlyn put her arm around her aunt, kissing her cheek. Seamus had looked out for them all along.

Connor reached across Kaitlyn's legs and held Tillie's other hand.

Jack cleared his throat. "And, Tillie, if ye'd care to join me for a bit of coffee this mornin', I believe these two lovebirds have waited long enough for some alone time."

Connor stood.

Jack opened the door for Tillie and then followed

her out of the room.

Kaitlyn didn't miss the look that passed between the two men. When the door closed, Kaitlyn scooted over, patting the space next to her.

Connor sat back beside her. He swung his feet up onto the bed and leaned back against the pillows, wrapping his arms around her and laying her head on his chest. "Katie, there's somethin' I'd ask ye."

His voice rumbled beneath her ear. "Okay." She tightened her insides, worried about what would come next.

"I know we've not spent much time together since ye arrived in Ireland, and the time we have spent has been full of confusion and misunderstandin' for both of us. But nearly losin' ye again made me a different man, and I'll not wait. I want ye to marry me, Katie." He pulled a ring out of his pocket and slid it on her finger.

She gasped, lifting her hand and studying the claddagh design of a crown above two hands clasping a heart. From Aunt Tillie, Kaitlyn knew the symbol represented loyalty, friendship, and love and was a traditional Irish wedding ring.

"'Tis only temporary," Connor said. "I'll buy a diamond or anythin' ye want, I just—"

A thrill moved through her, filling her with warmth and scattering the last bit of worry. Katie sat up and twisted to face him, pressing her finger against his lips. A tear slipped down her cheek. "Of course, I'll marry you, Connor. And the ring is perfect. But...you *will* have to wait."

Connor reached to wipe away the tear with his thumb. He raised his eyebrows.

"I've always dreamed of wearing the cutest shoes I

can find to my wedding. Right now, my feet are swollen and covered in bandages."

Connor grinned. "Aye, and 'tis probably best for my ribs to heal before our honeymoon. I'd rather not worry about my wife bringin' me to tears every time she puts her arms around me."

She grinned. "How would we look in our wedding pictures? You with stitches on your cheek, and me with a bandage around my head?"

"At least, we've matchin' bruises. Quite a color scheme, I'd say."

Kaitlyn rested her elbow on the pillow, her hand supporting her head, and traced Connor's lips with her finger. "Your wife? Hmm. I like the sound of that title." They would still have to figure out so many things. Her job, her house…but she pushed aside all of these thoughts to sort out later. Right now, all that mattered was she and Connor would be together.

Connor pulled her face to his, pausing a breath away. "'Tis somethin' I'd never imagined callin' anyone else," he murmured against her lips. "Though I took these many years to realize it, Katie. My Katie. Always 'twas ye."

Epilogue

Connor carried his suitcase up the Manor House steps. He paused for a moment and pulled off a Celtic knot pendant hanging on a ribbon from the door handle. He studied it before sliding it into his pocket. The charm clinked against the one he'd found dangling from his rearview mirror when he'd climbed into his car at the airport a few hours earlier.

He stepped across the threshold and breathed a sigh of relief. He was home at last. Three entire weeks instructing new recruits at a training camp was a long time for a man to be away from his new wife of only six months. He'd missed Katie fiercely, and his heart beat faster at the thought of hurryin' up the stairs and climbin' into bed next to her.

Stepping onto the stairs, he saw the last knot tied to the wooden railing. He glanced up the stairs once before he untied it. He pursed his lips, a bit frustrated at having to wait to see Katie. Obviously, she'd something planned and, knowing his wife, he wouldn't be disappointed if he followed the game once again. He expertly attached the knots together, and walking to the statue, knelt down, and shoved the key into place.

Lord Angus's leg detached.

Connor caught it, turning it over. A small package fell out. He picked it up, thinking it better contain a negligée or a cute pair of lacy knickers when he turned it over and saw the tag attached. On it was written a single word: *Da*. With shaking fingers, he untied the ribbon and tore off the paper. In his hands he held two miniature sets of baby stockings. He stilled, his throat constricting and, hearing a sound, he looked up.

Katie stepped from the shadows beneath the stairs.

He rushed to her, pulling her into his arms and searched her face for any indication of how she felt. "Katie, is it true?"

Her eyes glistened in the low glow of the hall lights as she nodded. "I found out for sure a few weeks ago, but the news wasn't the kind of thing you tell over the phone."

He looked her over but couldn't discern a difference. "And…two?"

Katie nodded again, she grimaced. "Are you happy? I mean twins are a surprise, and—"

"'Tis terrified I am, yet my heart's singin', Katie." He pushed a hand into her hair, pulling her mouth to his. The taste of her, the feel, was so comforting, and he couldn't imagine his life without Katie waiting at home for his return. He pulled her harder against him as his lips reacquainted themselves with hers.

She pulled away, taking a step back.

He placed a hand on her belly which was still flat as he'd remembered, and he studied her. He'd have to control the wave of anxiety he felt as they opened this new chapter in their lives. "Am I hurtin' ye, Katie?"

She moved close, her eyes darkening. A smile curled on her lips as she slid her hand down his arm to hold his. "No. I'd just like you to continue this upstairs—where you can take your time about it."

A word about the author...

I graduated with a degree in Linguistics from the University of Utah, and I taught English as a Second Language until I became a mom.

Now, I have four boys who keep me running all the time.

While I enjoy motherhood, I find my escape to the world of reading and writing crucial to my sanity.

The Sheik's Ruby was my first attempt at writing an entire novel, and it took nearly three years of attending writers' conferences, joining a critique group—and then another, reading, and studying to finally finish it.

I enjoy travel—especially spending time in the Middle East and Europe.

http://www.authorjmoore.com

Other titles by the author:
A Change of Heart
Safe Harbor
The Sheik's Ruby

Thank you for purchasing
this publication of The Wild Rose Press, Inc.

For questions or more information
contact us at
info@thewildrosepress.com.

The Wild Rose Press, Inc.
www.thewildrosepress.com

To visit with authors of
The Wild Rose Press, Inc.
join our yahoo loop at
http://groups.yahoo.com/group/thewildrosepress/